D0262610

SIX FOR LARAMIE

Six gun-fighters come to Laramie — all hungry for money. Yet greed is not everyone's sole motive. Bannerman, the toughest and fastest, has a special reason: one of the other five has shot his friend in the back. There's no charge for what he intends to do to him, even though he knows this might disrupt the plans for the work he's been hired to do — and that it could put him on the wrong end of *five* guns!

RICK DALMAS

SIX FOR LARAMIE

Complete and Unabridged

LINFORD
Leicester

First published in Great Britain in 2009 by
Robert Hale Limited
London

First Linford Edition
published 2010
by arrangement with
Robert Hale Limited
London

British Library CIP Data

Dalmas, Rick.
   Six for Laramie.- -(Linford western stories)
   1. Western stories.
   2. Large type books.
   I. Title II. Series
   823.9'2–dc22

ISBN 978–1–44480–397–6

Published by
F. A. Thorpe (Publishing)
Anstey, Leicestershire

Set by Words & Graphics Ltd.
Anstey, Leicestershire
Printed and bound in Great Britain by
T. J. International Ltd., Padstow, Cornwall

This book is printed on acid-free paper

Prologue

The Pass

There was more gunsmoke than that which was rolling up from the prairie fire burning three miles away out on the plains.

It wasn't supposed to be this way, but Wiley, trigger-happy as usual, had set it off by opening fire as the pack train of seven mules and mostly Mexican outriders started into the narrow pass.

The plan had been to allow them to get smack in the middle before firing a few warning shots, then to close off both ends of the pass. But, no, Wiley couldn't hold back; he was fascinated by the flash of sunlight from the brass in the bullet belts crossing the barrel chest of the lead rider.

It drew him like a target with a hundred-dollar prize for the man who could hit a bull's eye.

Wiley's bullet smashed home and, even as the big Mexican toppled, one or two of the cartridges in the belts exploded. That was what started the panic: the riders wheeling, firing blind at the rim of the pass, all looking for the attackers. The mules were abandoned, left to mill and snort and bray, harness jangling, wondering what in hell had happened.

The outfit had to follow Wiley's lead now. They rose to their feet and began pouring lead down into the dust-clouded chaos in the pass below. Benedict and Tim Willard hit the saddle and rode to cut off the riders right at the entrance to the pass. Three had already broken away and, though shooting back as they went — without aiming — had no intention of sticking around.

But the uniformed soldiers were being harangued by a red-faced *teniente*, the man waving a sabre in one hand, a pistol in the other. Then suddenly he

2

slumped and spilled untidily out of the saddle, shot between the eyes. Wiley smiled crookedly to himself as he levered another shell into his smoking Winchester, beaded a running soldier and hit him in the back of the head, which exploded like a melon.

Tim Willard was startled to be jumped by a Mexican leaping from a rock. The man grappled with him and for a few moments they struggled on the whickering, swerving mount. Then the horse stopped suddenly and they fell to the ground, still trying to kill each other. Tim got a knee into a fat belly, turned his head away from the gust of garlic and *vino* and rammed a rigid arm across the man's throat. He bared his teeth as he put weight on it, felt the larynx crush, and the violent convulsions of the strangling man. He kept the pressure on until the man was still, horses and mules stomping and running around him. He sat back on his knees, panting, looked up as he saw Wiley jumping down from a rock and running towards him.

Wiley gestured to the dead Mexican in front of Tim and nodded approval. Tim's reddened eyes moved towards his victim — and he didn't see Wiley's rifle swing in towards him. He felt the slamming of the bullet between his shoulders as he was driven violently forward, across the Mexican's body. Through a fading red haze, he saw Wiley reloading the rifle, looking around him, hawking in the thick powdersmoke and dust. Then Tim passed out, wondering why the hell Wiley had shot him . . .

There were three more of the original gang still alive, and the gunfire was dwindling now. Then it picked up: five fast rifle shots and the three robbers collapsed where they stood, all shot from behind.

A sweating Todd Benedict came riding back, waving.

'That's all of the Mexes, Wiley. How we doin' . . . ?' The words trailed off as he saw his companions sprawled amongst the dead. 'Judas priest! What happened . . . ? I thought we had the upper hand . . . '

'That damn lieutenant whipped his men into a frenzy, nailed our boys like a row of skittles . . . Goddamn! Was just too late to stop one of 'em puttin' a bullet into Tim!'

Benedict blinked, his face pale beneath the dirt and smeared gun-smoke. 'Judas!' he breathed again, shaking his head. Then he jumped from his horse and ran towards where Tim Willard lay, one leg moving. 'Tim's still alive!'

Wiley spun as Benedict knelt beside the backshot man — but it was no use.

Willard was too far gone. His blood-spattered lips moved and Benedict leaned down to hear.

He looked up slowly, frowning, as he rose to his feet.

'He — he cussed you to hell and the Devil, Wiley! With his dyin' breath. Why would he do that?'

Wiley shrugged. 'I dunno. I thought

Tim an' me got along pretty good — same as me and you.'

Not true! Benedict told himself silently. Wiley didn't 'get along' very well with anyone. The man was too self-centred, too ruthless, uncaring. But he had to admit there had been no open hostility — just a lack of camaraderie.

Shaking his head in puzzlement, he looked at the mules huddling together now in a corner of the rocky pass. He gestured towards their dusty leather packs.

'Well, looks like a good haul.'

'Just the two of us to split it now.'

Benedict looked sharply at Wiley, then back to the dead Willard. He stared a long moment, turned back towards his horse.

'Coupla mules still outside the pass. I'll go haze 'em in.'

'Yeah. I better start diggin' a few graves.' But Wiley Satterlee didn't set down his rifle as Benedict swung into leather and started to ride back down the pass.

He was almost to the entrance when Wiley threw his rifle up to his shoulder, sighted quickly, and fired.

Benedict was jarred forward in the saddle by the bullet, somewhere down in his lower back. He dropped his own rifle, almost falling, clung desperately to the horse's mane. He somehow managed to jam in the spurs, and set it running out of the pass as he clung desperately to the saddle-horn.

Behind him, Wiley's rifle thundered in a ragged volley.

1

Last Man

Heath Bannerman was the last of them to arrive in town.

Slouched easily in the saddle, he allowed his dusty roan to make its own pace down Main Street, unheeding of the chaotic traffic. If he heard the expletives and insults flung his way by the drivers of wagons or buckboards forced to go round him, he showed no sign of it.

A few soldiers from the fort sprawled in the shade of awnings, paying him minimal attention. Some of the regular cracker-barrel set, lounging on the raised boardwalk outside the general store on the corner, gave him more than a passing glance: another stranger — this made six. In a week!

Maybe they saw something more in him than they'd found in the other five who had drifted in. Something similar, yet different, with a harder edge, giving an impression that here was a spring coiled, ready for release: a spring, or something more deadly — like a diamondback, or a cougar about to pounce on its prey.

There was enough of the big cat about Bannerman's demeanour to make a couple of the loafers shift position a little — just a little, for a better view. But if they'd been a shade more energetic, say, enough to back-track him a short distance, out to the edge of the Medicine Bows, now no more than a mist-blue series of humps against the sky, they might have found the faint traces of a camp on the highest accessible ridge. To an experienced eye, there would be enough sign to reveal that one man had been camped here for a few days, possibly a week. The position gave an excellent view of every trail leading into Laramie.

The conclusion must be that some-one had been mighty wary, staying hidden while he checked riders heading into the town, before deciding to ride in himself.

There had been five of them this past week, one a day, skip Sunday — and today was Monday. Bannerman, drifter number six, was two days late, but the loungers couldn't know that.

For a stranger, though, he seemed to know his way around — or had been given very clear and detailed directions.

His first stop was at Joel Addison's, the town gunmaker. Dismounted and standing on the walk, dusting his ordinary range clothes with his hat, he stood just under six feet tall, hair plastered to his head, sweat-darkened, a deep brown, with a suggestion of pepper and salt sprinkled at the temples. He held his hat in his left hand, slapping it in brief, jerky motions, lifting a strange milky-red cloud of dust — a colour only found in one section of the Medicine Bows.

He moved easily, jamming his hat back on and sliding a long-barrelled rifle from a weathered saddle scabbard. A couple of folk made way for him as he entered the gunshop.

He emerged again in about twenty minutes, still carrying the rifle, but it gleamed with a coating of gun oil now and the brightness of a new blued-metal hood covering the foresight, protecting it from damage which could throw off the shooter's aim. Someone counted three boxes of bullets as he dropped them into his saddle-bag, sheathed the rifle and led the roan towards the livery stable. This stood one street back from Main, not readily seen, but he seemed to know just where to find it. *Maybe he had been here before* . . .

After giving orders for his mount to be taken care of, Bannerman walked back to Main, carrying rifle and warbag, and entered the Grand Hotel through the etched-glass double doors. The clerk came more alert as Bannerman approached and spoke his name. The clerk checked a list, held down by a corner of the heavy register, nodded as he looked at the hard-muscled lean-ness of the man waiting patiently. He averted his gaze from the sober, stubbled face with the steady grey-green eyes, noted the six-gun carried almost care-lessly, the holster pushed around towards the back of the hip. This surprised the clerk — though he was relieved, too — but he had expected to see the gun slung low in a tied-down holster. *Like the other men on the list . . .*

'Room Nine, Mr Bannerman,' he said pleasantly reaching down a key. 'Right opposite the head of the stairs — as requested,' Ideal for a fast getaway . . .

'Gimme a few minutes, then send up a bath and lots of hot water. I'll have some laundry to be done, too.'

'Certainly, sir.' The words were polite but as the new arrival turned towards the stairs the clerk scowled; three of the others had tipped him, but he had to admit this Bannerman looked different, somehow — like he knew exactly what he wanted, and was used to getting it.

He might have passed for just a tough drifter — the others had worn their guns in various ways, all of which spoke of 'gunfighter'. But his room had been reserved right along with the others so he *had* to be part of that group, whoever they were, and whatever the hell they were up to in Laramie — butt-end of the world as far as the clerk was concerned. He was only working here because the Grand was a family-run business and his father had given him two choices: 'Henry, learn the ropes of managing the hotel — or ride out and don't bother coming back.' Some goddamn choice!

Feeling heaps better after the long soak in the sudsy bath, fresh-shaved, hair trimmed and smelling of bay rum, Heath Bannerman was sitting on the edge of the bed, in his clean, but wrinkled clothes, tugging on his newly polished riding-boots, when the door opened. All he saw was enough blonde curls to stuff a cornsack, lips as red as a sunset, gleaming teeth in a wide smile — and lots of white flesh on bared shoulders. A swirl of green silk dress was apparently held up only by a pair of breasts showing an almost indecent amount of cleavage. A ready-for-fun voice said brightly, in a Southern drawl, 'Howdy — I'm Randy!'

'I'm not. Try your luck a little later on, sis.'

The smile disappeared and she went very still, about five-feet-three inches of outraged, hair-trigger whore. ' 'Try my luck!' he says! You have a damned high opinion of yourself, drifter! Who d'you think you are — Casanova?'

'Distant kin, my pa always claimed.' He spoke as he crossed the room and took one of her soft white arms, turning her to face out of the room. 'I'll let you know if I want you.'

'Well, don't do me no favours!' She ran cool, narrowed eyes over him, scalp to toes, let her pliant body fall against him, wriggling enticingly. 'You're nothing special.'

'Makes two of us.'

She struggled to get free, lifting a hand with a small ready fist, then abruptly stopped. Her face changed. 'Don't throw me out!' There was a plea behind those pale eyes now. 'She'll be mad and I'll never work in this town again . . . '

'She?'

'You know who I mean!'

He shrugged, pushing her out more gently. 'Cheyenne's a better deal for you, anyway. Go to Cirque Femme on Randolph Street, and tell Madame de Ville I sent you.'

Her eyes widened. 'You know — *her*?'

'Was married to her once. Good luck, Randy.'

He closed the door and lowered the shades, sprawled on the bed, his six-gun on the chair beside it, and closed his eyes.

He awoke to a pounding on the door. He scooped up the six-gun even as he swung his legs over the side of the mattress, the gun's hammer spur under his thumb. 'Who is it?'

A woman's voice answered and at first he thought maybe Randy had returned, but the voice said,

'Mr Bannerman, I'm Mariah Bird-wood. I'd like to speak with you.'

'Go stand right at the head of the stairs. No closer. Call out when you get there.'

'Who d'you think you're talking to?'

'You're the one wanted to talk. If you still do, call out when you're at the top of the stairs, otherwise, forget it.'

A short silence, brief footsteps, then the voice, very tight with outrage now, 'I'm at the top of the stairs.'

'Stay put.'

He unlocked the door, making plenty of noise with the iron key, then wrenched it open, using the door as a shield, only the gun's barrel showing around the edge.

'What the . . . ?' The startled words came from a big, heavy-set man who had apparently been standing, flattened against the wall beside the door. He had obviously expected Bannerman to step into the hallway. Now he moved fast, trying to make up for time already lost, one heavy fist rising as he took a step forward. 'Get back in there . . . '

As he tried to bull his way into the room, Bannerman slammed the door with full force. There was a solid thump, a grunt, and the sounds of staggering as the man hurtled back across the width of the landing. Bannerman glimpsed a woman as she dodged quickly out of the way of the flailing arms, then the man was clattering and bouncing and somer-saulting down the stairs, shaking the whole kit and caboodle.

Bannerman saw an angry, oval face, shoulder-length black hair spilling from under a narrow-brimmed hat, eyes blazing. 'What d'you think you're doing!'

He stepped to one side, jerking his head in a 'come on in' gesture that only served to make her angrier.

'Put that gun away!' she snapped,

pushing past him.

'Not yet.' He was watching the stairs. The man who had just tumbled down and was now bleeding from the nose, above one eye and a corner of his cursing mouth, pulled himself up by the banister. He lumbered on to the landing and launched himself at Bannerman, who stepped to one side and clubbed him behind the ear with his gun. The man fell, his impetus carrying him halfway into the room as he stretched out in the doorway. Bannerman kicked his legs aside and started to close the door. He paused when he saw the hesitant clerk halfway up the stairs, mouth-breathing as he asked in a croaking voice,

'Is — everything all right, Miss Birdwood?'

'It will be, thank you, Henry.' She closed the door, looking steadily at Bannerman. 'Won't it, Mr Bannerman?'

'Seems that way.' He gestured to the room's only easy chair and dropped on to the edge of the bed again. She stood, watching him. He smiled crookedly as he slid the pistol back into the holster. 'You can put away that derringer too.'

She flushed and slid the small gun she had been holding in the folds of her skirt behind her wide belt. 'I hardly expected to need a gun just to visit a man I'd sent for.'

'That toy wouldn't've been enough to stop me putting a bullet into you.'

She frowned. 'I'm not sure it was such a good idea — sending for you. I don't know that I can use a man with such a short fuse.'

'Just don't like people pointing guns at me.'

She smiled thinly. 'You find it . . . uncomfortable, being on the wrong end of a gun?'

'Sure. How about you?' He flicked the holster and she realized he was still gripping the six-gun.

She started to rise. 'Look, I've had enough of this. I'll give you two hundred dollars, you can stay the night in this room, and then — well, then I'm afraid I don't give a damn what happens to you.'

She reached into a deep pocket in her buckskin riding-skirt and sucked down a sharp breath as he unsheathed the gun and snapped the hammer back to full cock.

'I hope you only aim to bring out your wallet.'

She released a breath, taking her hand — empty — from the pocket. 'A very careful man!'

He nodded. 'It's five hundred you owe me, not two.'

She flushed, eyes sparking. 'You son of a bitch! Don't you try to shake me down. It was five hundred for coming to Laramie to work for me! Not to throw my man down a flight of stairs and hold a cocked pistol on me!'

He shrugged, lowered the hammer and leathered the gun, strapping on the rig while she fumed. Their eyes met.

'Five hundred.'

She stared at him malevolently, noting his nose, which had obviously been broken more than once in the past. The grey-green eyes were slightly mocking — *maddeningly mocking!* — the wide mouth showing some private amusement, which she knew damn well she was providing for him! The rugged jaw spoke of determination. *More like stubbornness for this jackass!* she decided silently.

He was a confident man — confident he could cope with any situation that arose. *Exactly the kind of man she needed for this job! But . . . .*She flushed a little as she realized he was looking at her just as speculatively as she was watching him.

He saw she was quite tall, a couple of inches shorter than he was, deeply tanned from frequent exposure to the Wyoming sun and the elements in general. She was obviously a working ranch woman, rich, or, at least, had access to plenty of cash. She had probably offered the other five the same deal of $500 appearance money, a first-class hotel room, at least overnight, with all amenities, if Randy was anything to judge by, apparently paid for by Mariah Birdwood. In any case, he knew about her large ranch, the Crown: her father had taken the term 'Cattle King' seriously and constantly reminded folk of his status with his choice of brand. Seemed to Bannerman that some of her father's arrogance and self-belief had rubbed off on Mariah.

'All right!' she said suddenly, dropping back into the easy chair. 'Five hundred. I'll stand by my word.'

'So you should.'

'You stand by yours, of course!'

'You already know that or you wouldn't've sent for me.'

'I — don't like your attitude much, Bannerman.'

'I'm not selling it.' He slapped a hand against his six-gun, making her tense momentarily. '*This* is what you're buying. Or — is it?' He looked carefully at her now. He shook his head briefly. 'Not 'it'. It's *guns*, isn't it? I recognized some of the others: Tony Ramirez, Josh

Caldwell and, maybe, Kid Shipley. I couldn't get a real good look at him.'

'You've been watching the others arrive? For how long? Damn you, Bannerman, you were supposed to get here on Saturday.'

'I did. Just waited up in the Medicine Bows before coming on down.'

'Watching who else I'd sent for. Well, I did hear you were mighty thorough and wary.'

He spread his hands. 'I'm here.'

'I take it you mean you're *still* here. Because you are careful. All right. I grant you that in your profession it is a necessary attribute. It's too bad that obeying orders doesn't seem to be another attribute where you're concerned.'

'Aw, I'll obey any order I figure is OK.'

'You figure is OK?'

'Sure. I'll give you full value for money, but the money has to be right.'

'I think . . . we're beginning to understand each other now, Mr Bannerman.'

'Don't be too sure.' He took out a

cheroot from a buffalo-hide case, its corners edged with silver, and lit up.

'Well? Are you ready to go to work?'

'If I've passed muster, and after we've gone through one small ritual that so far you've overlooked.'

A frown pinched her brow. 'Small? Oh! Your five hundred dollars!'

'That sounds right — now.'

She fumbled at her pocket and brought out a drawstring chamois poke, tossed it on to the bed. Coins clinked. He picked it up slowly, tugging at the leather drawstring. 'It's all there!'

'Once took a man's word for that — same kinda leather poke, same clinking sound. Except when I got back to my room, I found I was carrying a pokeful of washers — most of 'em rusted, too. Not even usable.'

She laughed, eyes flashing, as he spilled gold and silver coins on to the bedcovers. He swiftly counted them by sight as she got her laughter under control. He put the coins away, drew the bag tight and held it in his right hand, the cheroot in the other.

She smiled now, a warm, genuinely amused smile, softening her face: she wasn't beautiful, but she was quite handsome when she dropped her arrogant act: about twenty-five.

'Tony Ramirez, Kid Shipley, Josh Caldwell — and me. Who're the other two?'

'Do you need to know?'

'Who're the other two?'

'Why? Have they got to meet with your approval, too? You seem to forget I'm the one paying for all this.'

'I may not be a part of 'all this', whatever it is.'

'If you don't 'approve' of the men you have to work with?'

He nodded and she stared at him levelly. 'You must have damned good eyes to recognize anyone from back in those hills.'

'Good field glasses. German lenses. Once belonged to one of Maximilian's generals.'

Her eyes widened. 'You fought his

men? I've heard those French Foreign Legionnaires are . . . impressive, that the word 'surrender' isn't even in their vocabulary.'

'Dunno about that, but they're the toughest men I've ever had to fight. Juárez thought so, too. Who're the others?'

'You don't give up, do you!'

'Who are they?'

'Damn you, Bannerman!' She glared for so long that he opened his mouth, ready to ask again, and she blurted out, 'Jonas Flood and Wiley Satterlee.'

'Flood's OK — '

'*Thank* you! I'm sure I'll sleep better knowing you endorse my choice of the men I hire.'

'Yeah, Flood's OK, but Satterlee . . . ' He shook his head uncertainly. 'Never worked with him or even met him, for the matter of that, but I've heard some things about him I don't like.'

'Oh? You listen to gossip?'

'No, I listen to men I admire enough to trust. And two of them happened to be on a chore with this Satterlee. He left one for dead in the badlands, but he lived, he'll never walk again without a stick. The other died cursing Wiley with his last breath. No one ever knew who put the bullet in his back. Nor where his share of the loot went, but it was Satterlee who turned up in Dodge, with bulging saddle-bags, painted the town red, then moved on to Deadwood and . . . I haven't heard much about him since then.'

Her eyes narrowed with a sudden, unwanted, realization. 'You knew I'd sent for him, didn't you! For some reason, you're after Satterlee and . . . ' She stood abruptly, shaking her head. 'Oh, no! You settle your troubles on your own time, not when you're working for me. Yes! I think I see now! Well, my deal is five hundred appearance money, which I've already paid you, and the others. There'll be another two thousand dollars each when the job is finished.'

He nodded gently, made no comment.

'Look, Bannerman, I'll be blunt. You will not be told what the job is until you indicate you will agree to follow my orders *implicitly*. No short cuts, no compromises. You will do *exactly* as I say, no questions asked.'

'No.'

She drew herself up. 'What?'

'I don't work blind. If I can see a better and safer way of doing something I'll do it; if the same result is achieved in the end you won't have anything to gripe about.'

'No. This will be done my way, or not at all! I've spent too long planning it to have it jeopardized by . . . improvisation — and revenge, on time *I*'ve paid for.'

He shrugged. 'Then, in my case, I guess it's 'not at all'. I'm not that strapped for money that I'll sell my life for two thousand dollars.'

'But it's not that at all, is it? Your real problem is you don't like taking orders from a woman!'

'Hell, I can live with that, as long as the orders make sense — and are flexible.'

She stared, tight-lipped, a moment longer, then turned towards the door. 'There's nothing more to say.' She paused with her hand on the doorknob. 'Damn you, Bannerman! I was depending on you. You have a good reputation. Is this your way of holding me up for a bigger fee?'

'No. I told you how it is.'

She turned sharply, frowning at the door panel. She heard movements outside. Her man was coming round, it seemed. Smiling, she opened the door. 'It's all right, Casey, I'm all through here — and so are you. Go see Carlsen in the town office and draw your time.'

The groggy, blood-spattered Casey blinked. He was a big hulking, slow-thinking man. 'Draw my . . . time?' He rubbed at sticky blood behind his left ear. 'What for?'

'Well, look at you. You don't seem to have earned your pay, do you?'

Casey's jaw set hard and he flicked burning eyes to Bannerman. 'You never said he'd be that tough.'

'Well, now you know. *Leave*, Casey. Go find Nils Carlsen and pick up your money. And only take what's yours from the bunkhouse at Crown.'

Casey's glare shifted to Bannerman's expressionless face. 'I'll be in town a spell, mister!'

Bannerman said nothing as the man swung away so angry that he almost fell down the stairs, had to grab the rail to steady himself. He shook it in frustration.

'I see why you sent for outside help.'

She smiled mysteriously. 'Oh, Casey's just a roughneck, not as tough as he — or I — thought, it seems. You won't change your mind?'

'Will you change yours?'

She hesitated and he saw how hard it was for her to say her next words: 'I . . . might think about what you said. A little flexibility may be necessary. And you are a man with more experience than me in this sort of thing.'

'We could do a deal yet, then?'

'But make no mistake, Bannerman, you'll earn your money. Or I'll fire you just as quickly as I did Casey.'

2

I'll Buy The Drinks

Bannerman ate supper in the hotel dining room: an indifferent meal, but he wasn't a man who fussed over food. If it provided him with needed energy he was content.

After smoking a cheroot and reading the *Cheyenne Chronicle* in the foyer, where he was the centre of some covert attention — it seemed that Henry, the clerk, had spread the word that he had knocked Big Casey down the stairs — he settled his gun rig more comfortably and stepped out into the dusk.

There was a fine sunset over the Medicine Bows and he paused to admire it. He had always liked this time of day, between sundown and dark; it could be a lonely time for some men,

33

but he had thoughts aplenty to keep him company.

Main was still busy with traffic, both wheeled and the walking kind. It was a long time since he had been to Laramie. It had been smaller then and he had been using a different name. After seeing his face staring at him from a weathered Wanted dodger outside the post office, he had shaved off his close-cropped beard, and had his long, wild hair trimmed to a more presentable length and shape.

For the first time for years he went back to using his own name. He had used aliases long enough, so the family wouldn't have suffered on account of his deeds. Now there was only Sister Carmel left; he hoped his last letter had found her at that 'General Delivery' address in Wagon Mound, New Mexico.

He thought about her for a few minutes before moving on, the light fading slowly. The army's presence was still evident in Laramie, though he had heard the fort was only half-manned these days, now that the Indians were settling down.

He killed most of an hour strolling through town, looking in store windows. Fact was, it was a long time since he had been in a town anywhere near the size of Laramie. Then he found a medicine show on a vacant lot down a side street where the vocal drummer was apparently trying to pass himself off as a direct descendant of one of the disciples of Jesus.

Holding forth from his platform behind his laden wagon, he leaned into the scattered crowd, singling out one man dressed in range clothes.

'You have the time, friend, I can guide you through a genealogical trail that begins with my birth and leads directly back to the manger!' He held up a small clay jar with a pointed end. 'And why can I do that? Because I have a phenomonal memory — all because of this miraculous balm in a genuine antique miniature amphora, made from the clay of Israel. My friends, I call this 'miraculous' because it *is*! It not only aids the mind, cures most ailments and prolongs a man's . . . energy . . . in a certain direction . . . ' He winked with a slight leer and got a couple of catcalls from drunks, before continuing with his extravagant claims.

'Mebbe you better buy me a jar of that stuff,' a voice said beside Bannerman.

He turned his head, curious, had to raise his eyes slighty to see the battered face. 'Collect yourself a few bruises, Casey?'

Mariah Birdwood's ex-cowhand glared. There was a smell of liquor when he spoke again. 'I got lotsa bruises, thanks to you. An' no job — also thanks to you.'

'You just underestimated things, that's all.'

Casey frowned. 'You got the drop on me!'

'Someone'll always get the drop on you, Casey. You can't go up against a man with a gun and hope your size is gonna scare him long enough for you to knock his head off.'

Casey's frown deepened as he thought about it; the Jesus freak was still spouting in the background, really getting into his stride now. 'She never said you was a gunfighter.'

'Didn't you know about the others?'

'What others?'

Bannerman shrugged and started to move on but Casey grabbed him by the arm, fingers closing like a steel trap. 'I told you I'd be in town for a while.'

'And here you are. Casey, you don't let go my arm, I'll bust your head open.' He slapped a hand to his gun butt. 'You grabbed the wrong arm.'

'Aaaah.' The big man released his hold, swayed a little. He started to ball up a fist.

'Don't be loco. You can't hit me before I shoot you — or slug you out cold. C'mon. I'll buy you a drink.'

'Huh? Why? I still wanna knock your head off.'

'Well, you know what'll happen if you try. Come and have a few drinks instead. You might still have a sore head in the morning, but at least you'll wake up.'

Bannerman moved off, turning towards a saloon with a side door. He had reached it before he heard Casey lumbering after him.

'I know why you wanna buy me a drink. You're gonna gemme drunk and ask me all about that Birdwood bitch.'

'Well, figured you'd be riled at her, Casey. Might tell me a couple things I can use. Let's just have a couple of snorts and see what happens, eh?'

Bannerman took the big man's arm and had no trouble leading him into the saloon's smoky bar, the rumble of men's voices hitting them like a solid wave as they entered.

They found a table in a corner, quite a way from the bar, but Bannerman bought a bottle of bourbon. He insisted on one still in its wrapper, although that was no real guarantee the hooch hadn't been doctored. He refilled Casey's glass for the third time, saw the big, homely face starting to slacken, the eyes slowly glazing.

'How long you work for Crown?'

'Few years — on and off. Left a coupla times, then went back. Been there about a year 'n a half, this time. Started end of winter before last.'

'She's not a good boss?'

'Aw, s'pose she's OK. Knows cattle good as any man. 'Course old Darby Birdwood seen to that. She was his only kid, you know. Wife died soon after givin' birth, an' he never got the son he wanted, so Mariah had to stand in.'

'This would've happened long before you were there.'

'Sure. But there's a few old hands still there. Don't do much to earn their pay; think she keeps 'em on because ol' Darby wanted it that way. They like to put their feet up on the potbelly stove on cold nights, you know?'

'Yeah, a good time for talking.'

Casey filled his own glass again,

spilling some, licking it off his fingers before tossing the drink down.

'Darby used her, the old-timers say. Made her side him at all the fancy wingdings in Cheyenne, act as hostess for cattle buyers. Huh! Reckon she softened up plenty of lonely good old boys from prairie sod huts; sweetened many a good deal so it swung ol' Darby's way.' He winked and Bannerman was remembering his glimpse of that smile that transformed Mariah's face; yes, he saw how it could put a flutter in the heart of some rough, unmarried cowman from the wilds of Wyoming, and affect his judgement in a hard-trading cattle deal.

'He died a few years back, didn't he?'

'Yeah. Found him with a dozen Sioux arrers stickin' right through him.' Casey frowned, draining dregs from his glass, reaching for the bottle again. 'Old-timers always seem puzzled over that. There was whispers Darby had himself a Sioux woman, some say even a half-breed kid who stayed with the tribe — '

'There's always that kind of talk.'

'No, no, couple of the old boys was serious. Darby mostly got along OK with the Sioux, so why would they turn him into a pincushion?'

'If he had a woman maybe there was a Sioux man interested in her, too. Put him outta the picture for keeps.'

'Yeah! Could be. But they had the army look into it, a Colonel Greer. Him an' Darby was old friends. Greer's retired now. Says he ain't about to die — not till he finds out what really happened to old Darby. Hey, you're not drinkin'.'

'You're doing enough for both of us. No, go ahead, Casey. A couple of shots see me through.'

'We-ell — if you say so.'

'Keep the bottle.' Bannerman started to rise to his feet and and was aware of a sudden wave of quiet sweeping through the bar.

The crowd was opening out to make way for a tall man in brown corduroy

41

trousers, white shirt under a black vest, which had a brass star pinned to it.

Casey saw Bannerman's gaze going past him and turned in his chair, almost falling. 'Aw, that's just Pat Magraw — the sheriff.'

'Coming this way.'

Casey, busy refilling his glass, looked startled.

'Sit still, Casey!' the lawman said, his right hand sweeping up his Colt as he came up to the table. He flicked cold eyes towards Bannerman. 'You stay outta this.'

Bannerman spread his hands. 'Whatever you say, Sheriff. But what seems to be the trouble?'

Magraw reached for Casey with his left hand and dragged him out of his chair. It clattered as it fell and Casey swayed and staggered.

'Hey!'

'Come on! I ain't got all night.'

'Where? I — '

'You're going to jail, you lousy thief.'

Casey blinked and Bannerman asked

quietly, 'What's he stolen?'

'I told you to stay outta it.'

'You did. I just want to know what he's supposed to've stolen — and by the look of him, Casey does, too.'

Magraw scowled, shook Casey who was unsteady on his feet. 'Miss Birdwood fired him an' when he left he took some stuff didn't belong to him. Not the first time, neither. He's known as a sneak-thief.'

'I ain't! Whoever says that is a liar an' — '

'Shut up, Casey!' The sheriff lifted his gun threateningly.

'Sheriff, you told me to stay out of this, and I have. But I don't see any need to beat Casey's head in over some piffling thing you say he stole.'

Magraw's eyes narrowed. He was tall, not too broad, but looked fit and supple as a hickory whip, and unless Bannerman was mistaken, those bleak, close-set eyes meant there was a hard-nosed personality behind them.

'I wouldn't want you to think I'm

43

scared of you, Bannerman, 'cause I ain't. But I got my orders about Casey, none about you . . . ' He let it hang, turned back to Casey. 'You want me to cuff you?'

Casey shook his head and immediately stumbled.

'I'll lend a hand to get him down to your jail.' Bannerman offered. 'He needs to sleep it off.'

'Last time, mister — stay — outta — this! I'm arrestin' Casey for stealin' a set of silver salt-and-pepper shakers from Miz Birdwood. No use you hangin' your jaw like that, Casey, an' tryin' to look innocent. I found them shakers in your warbag out at your camp by the creek. Went lookin' for you soon's I got word from Mariah.'

Casey shook his head, only succeeding in making himself dizzy, and Bannerman steadied him.

'Strange thing for a man like Casey to steal.'

The lawman held Bannerman's gaze. 'He's stole all kindsa things from the cowhands — his *bunkmates*, for Chris'sakes!'

Casey lowered his gaze but said nothing.

'Who'd want to buy things like that?'

'Listen, Bannerman, I'm gettin' a bellyful of you. Casey here's a mighty large man but I reckon I could squeeze you into the cell with him — if you gonna keep pokin' your snoot in where it ain't wanted.'

Bannerman nodded gently. 'I can see I'm getting in your hair, Sheriff. OK. I'll stay put.'

'You better! Now, you comin', Casey?'

Casey looked appealingly at Bannerman who kept his face blank. Then he shrugged and offered an arm to Magraw. As they started to move off, he pulled back.

'Hey, can I take my bottle?'

The sheriff swore, half-dragged the man towards the batwings. Bannerman watched them go, Then he had another drink and offered the remains of the bottle to a trio of cowpokes at the next table. One of them lunged for it in case Bannerman changed his mind.

'Thanks, amigo. We'll drink your health.'

'Maybe you ought to drink to Casey's,' Bannerman said quietly as he started out.

The trio frowned after him, puzzled, then they held out their glasses to the man with the bottle. 'Fill 'em up, Dix!'

★   ★   ★

The man was good.

Bannerman didn't see him or even sense his presence until he walked his mount out from the thicket, cocked carbine pointing at the gunfighter.

'You have to be Bannerman.'

The gunfighter reined up, keeping his hands in sight but not releasing the reins. The man with the gun looked like a cowpoke, even wearing scratched and scuffed working-chaps. He was about forty, lean-jawed, and the knotted muscles of his jawbone moved as he chewed, sideburns rippling. He spat a short brown stream to the left, without taking his eyes off Bannerman.

'You're late — and she ain't happy.'

'Longer you keep me here, the unhappier she'll get, most likely.'

The man grinned, showing teeth yellow and dark with tobacco juice. 'She can be a hellcat when she's riled — but you never heard that from me. Come on, I'll take you up to the house.'

Bannerman glanced past the thicket and saw the roof of the big, sprawling ranch house just beyond a rise about a half-mile away. 'Reckon I can find my way.'

'She'd be wastin' her money if you couldn't. I'll ride along to make sure you get there.'

They started towards the distant house, the man riding slackly, at ease, the butt of the carbine resting on his right thigh. The hammer was still back at full cock.

'Dangerous riding with a gun cocked like that.'

'Only for you.'

Bannerman smiled thinly. 'Mighty cautious. You got a name?'

'Dakota.'

'Good as any. The others here?'

'For a coupla, three hours. You ain't gonna be popular.'

Bannerman was sober now. 'No. Got held up — by a funeral.'

Dakota looked at him sharply, narrowed his eyes a little. 'They can drag on, some of 'em. Deacon Fields in Laramie, likes to throw in half the Bible in his services.'

'No Deacon. Just the undertaker said a few words.'

Dakota's frown deepened. 'I guess that's all you're gonna tell me. huh?'

Bannerman didn't answer and they made the rest of the ride in silence.

The house seemed to cover half the slope of the mountain. It was single-storeyed and had lots of covered verandas, even extra wide shelters over the doors. Built of timber, with riverstone fireplaces, of course — three that he could see, and a narrow flagged path ran all round the building. The roof was pitched more sharply than usual, no doubt to cope with the bone-numbing blizzards in this part of the country and the heavy layers of snow they deposited.

Mariah Birdwood was waiting on the big side porch, at the end nearest the front of the house. Even as they rode up the slope, Bannerman could see she was tight-lipped with impatience, her arms stiff where they leaned on the rail.

'Don't you have a watch? Or even a calendar!' she snapped.

'Sorry. Unavoidable delay.'

She moved jerkily and Dakota spat, saying, 'Had to go to a funeral . . . he says.'

That brought the woman up straight. Deep vertical lines appeared between her eyes as she stared at the dismounting gunfighter.

'I wouldn't've thought you knew

anyone in Laramie well enough to attend their funeral.'

Standing at the foot of the porch steps, he nodded.

'Didn't know him well, but there weren't many mourners. Big Casey.'

'What!'

'Magraw arrested him, on your orders apparently, for stealing some trivial thing — '

'Trivial be damned! They were a set of silver salt-and-pepper shakers my great-grandfather brought with him from England! They're over three hundred years old.'

'Casey would've been a fool to steal them, then, wouldn't he? Everyone around here would know they were yours. He'd never have been able to sell them.'

She waved a hand irritably. 'He wasn't all that smart — '

'And now he's dead.'

'What . . . happened?'

'According to Magraw he found him lying on his bunk. He'd been sick and the sheriff says he was afraid he might choke so went in to help. Casey was playing possum, jumped the sheriff but Magraw managed to get his gun out and it went off during the struggle — according to Magraw.'

She was breathing a little more quickly now, her face set in sober lines. 'You keep saying 'according to Magraw' as if you don't believe him.'

'I don't.'

'You don't even know the man! Pat Magraw is a good lawman, has a big reputation up here.'

'And does what he's told. Which must be nice, having a lawman on side.'

'What the hell does that mean?'

Bannerman stared back, remained silent.

Dakota coughed and the woman snapped her gaze to him. 'All right. You can go back to your chores, Dakota.' Then she looked at Bannerman again. 'And you'd better come on in. The others are waiting to meet you.'

'Why'd you bring Casey with you

when you came to meet me?'

She paused in turning towards the house door. Her gaze was cool. 'He happened to be in town on a ranch chore. I-I just thought I'd like someone with me when — you and I met. I intended to bawl you out for being late.'

Bannerman stared. 'My reputation scare you?'

She bristled. 'I too like to play things . . . carefully. Casey was big, but dumb. My mistake.'

'Mebbe dumb enough to talk about things he'd seen and heard on Crown? Things he oughtn't to talk about . . . ?'

'You're treading on very thin ice, Bannerman!'

'Been there before. You'd've done better to bring Dakota with you. Then Casey might still be alive.'

'Oh, to hell with you and your damn theories. Dakota had other chores, if you must know. Now, are you coming?'

3

Hired Guns

It was a big room at the rear of the house and five men sat in varying degrees of relaxation in straightback chairs around a large table that was scarred from years of use.

This was probably where once Darby Birdwood, and now Mariah, held ranch conferences to discuss the work projects on the spread, check tally books and so on. There were piles of ragged notebooks stacked in one corner, old, yellowed magazines tumbled in a heap nearby, some saddle gear pushed carelessly against the wall, a few shelves with nothing much on them gathering dust, and one tall wall cupboard with a warped door, but a padlock and hasp.

There was nothing cheerful or welcoming about this room. The chairs weren't even comfortable — maybe by design.

Five pairs of eyes turned to Bannerman as he entered, the girl stepping aside and sweeping a casual arm around the table, nodding towards Bannerman.

'This is Bannerman. Working from the top and going left: Tony Ramirez, Jonas Flood, Kid Shipley, Josh Caldwell and, last but not least, Wiley Satterlee.'

Bannerman nodded, sliding his eyes around the gunfighters in the order Mariah had introduced them.

Ramirez he had seen before in Mexico. He was a slim Mexican-American, not too handsome but with a charm (so they said) that could make a novice nun shed her habit. He lifted a finger where his hand rested on the edge of the table.

Jonas Flood was a worried-looking man in his mid-twenties, with hair parted in the middle, but still showing his widow's peak. His eyes crinkled as he smiled briefly. Next to him was Kid

Shipley. He was big, looked gawky, but Bannerman knew he was snake-fast with that long-barrelled Frontier Colt he wore in a cutaway holster, butt foremost. He didn't even bother looking up at Bannerman, but drank from his glass of whiskey and refilled it from one of the open bottles on the table. 'We've met,' he grated, without interest.

Josh Caldwell was pleasant-faced, about thirty, wore a frontier moustache which he had a habit of stroking — right before he drew and killed his man. He smiled, on-off, and nodded for good measure.

Bannerman let his gaze rest on Satterlee. Likely the oldest of the group, Satterlee looked mean and tough. Long dark hair hanging to his collar, he wore a battered brown hat with a punched-in crown tilted to the back of his head. He had a boot resting on the only available chair at the table.

'Find a chair and sit down, Bannerman. Been lookin' forward to meetin' you.'

'And me you.'

'Heard about me?'

'Few things. Mostly what Todd Benedict told me. And I heard Tim Willard died cursing your name.'

Satterlee smiled thinly. 'Yeah, Tim was kind of a knothead, worryin' all the time, couldn't decide if he really wanted to do a job or not.'

'Tim's dead. But Todd Bendict's still alive.'

'So I hear. Gets round in a wheelchair or somethin'.' There was no real interest in the query.

'Wheelchair's next. Uses crutches right now.'

Satterlee grunted. 'Too bad. Todd was OK. Little too many 'ethics' as he called 'em, but he'd square up to a grizzly with a butter-knife.'

Bannerman stood beside the chair where Satterlee's boot rested. 'Looks like the only chair left.'

Wiley's heavy eyebrows shot up in innocent surprise. 'Well, hell, so 'tis.' He struggled more upright, watching

Bannerman's expressionless face, then widened his smile and dropped his boot, nudging out the chair. 'Here, sit you down next to me. We can get to know each other.'

'Not while the meeting's on,' Mariah said from her own chair at the head of the table. She was shuffling a few papers, looked up and ran her gaze around the band of gunfighters. 'You've all been paid your five hundred dollars for coming?' There were nods, one or two grunts of acknowledgement. 'All right — moving on, this job I want you to do will pay two thousand dollars a head — or more.'

She paused, smiled slowly when she saw she definitely had their attention now.

'How much more?' Satterlee asked.

'That I'm not sure of. But a minimum two thousand dollars. *Minimum* I promise you.'

'You're the paymaster,' spoke up Caldwell in a surprisingly rough voice. 'You oughta know how much.'

'I guarantee you at least two thousand dollars each. Surely that's good enough? Whatever you make after that is a bonus. And, believe me, it could be a very big one.'

'Or not,' commented Kid Shipley, his big, pockmarked nose twitching some.

'Whatever it is, it'll be more than the money you were offered — and agreed to.'

Her gaze was steady, moving from man to man, pausing on Bannerman.

'I was on a deal like this once, down in Mexico, where such deals are more common than not. We had to pull a raid on a hacienda of a Governor whom Juárez's rebels wanted ousted. We were told the Governor's safe was stuffed to overflowing with gold and cash and we could divide it amongst us. No cash up front. This the same sort of deal?'

Mariah's face looked tighter now. She fiddled with her papers, aware that they were all watching her now. Then she lifted her pale face and looked around the table slowly.

'I will tell you this: we will be holdin up a train.' That news brought a few murmurs and shifting positions on the hard chairs. 'I don't believe any of you will have any problem with that?' No replies, so she continued. 'The train will include an express car with a large, special safe built in. What I want is in that safe. My information is that there will be several payrolls for army posts, totalling at least twelve thousand dollars — but possibly, even likely, a good deal more. It seems the army has been tardy in meeting its wages' obligations and Congress has finally ordered the back payments to be made. Now, I'll leave it to your imaginations to decide how much this may amount to — but I'm sure you'll agree it'll very probably be a lot more than twelve thousand dollars. Perhaps closer to twenty thousand.'

She sat back and awaited reactions.

'We bust the safe, and what's in it is ours — that it?' said Caldwell, an edge of excitement in his voice now.

Mariah shook her head. 'No, the

money is yours. Nothing else. We have to get that straight right now. *All* the money. That's it.'

That seemed satisfactory.

'A big special safe, you said,' Bannerman ventured. 'I guess we have to bust into that safe before we get anything.'

'Of course. There will be no keys for it on the train. An army officer will ride on ahead from fort to fort and open it only for the amount due to that particular fort.'

'That train ain't gonna be able to get near many forts,' spoke up Kid Shipley. 'They're too scattered and there ain't that much track laid down.'

'No. Where the rails run a good distance from the fort, the train'll be met by an army escort to take the payroll back.'

'Wouldn't that be a good time to hit 'em? Rather than hold up the train?' asked Jonas Flood.

Mariah was already shaking her head before he finished his query. 'No. There are still plenty of wild Indians on the loose and a lot of desperadoes hide out up here. The escort will be big and well-armed. The train will have only a small squad on board; they don't want to advertise too much that this is a special run.'

'There will be passenger cars, *señorita*?' Tony Ramirez spoke in his quiet, smooth voice that had had many a maiden almost swooning.

Not Mariah Birdwood. She looked at him coolly. 'One passenger car, possibly two.'

The men thought it over. Bannerman ran his eyes over the group once more and nodded to himself: she had chosen her wild bunch well.

He and Shipley had both had a lot of experience holding up trains, likely Ramirez, too, as most of it was done down in Mexico, fighting as soldiers of fortune for Juárez.

Caldwell was an ex-miner, an explosives expert.

Jonas Flood was a man who had

planned his jobs meticulously and had hired out his expertise in such services many a time.

And Satterlee — well, Satterlee was ruthless, the one who would get rid of guards or anyone — or anything — that endangered the job's success.

And all had a certain reputation as gunfighters.

Yes, Mariah Birdwood had gathered around her one of the most dangerous groups this country had ever seen.

And he wondered how she had come by such intimate information about that special pay-train. There would be little publicity about such a train; the army would keep it under wraps as tightly as they could.

But, of course, there was always someone privy to such information who had a price. Always.

★   ★   ★

There were two big bunkhouses and a long covered dogrun where the large crew sat down for meals and general relaxation. The cookhouse was linked to the bunkhouses by the dogrun. There seemed to be four kitchen staff.

As the hired guns learned at lunch-time, the crew of Crown ate well. It was better grub than Bannerman had tasted in many hotels that were supposed to use chefs with world-wide reputations. After the meal the crew returned to work, not without a lot of open staring at the gunfighters.

The group lingered over smokes. Bannerman leaned against an awning post, looking out over the vast pastures. He was aware of someone coming up beside him, glanced around as a big hand scraped a vesta down the rough bark of the post. Satterlee dipped his cigarette into the flame, shook the flame out and flicked the dead match away.

'You knew Todd Benedict, huh?'

'Know him,' Bannerman corrected.

'Uh-huh. Rode with him a coupla times.'

'Last time was when he caught a

bullet in the back.'

'Yeah — them Mexes. He tell you about that mule train we stopped in the Two-Step Pass? All them greasers, been livin' up here on the smell of a sweat-rag, scrabblin' around and damn if they don't hit on a bonanza.' He spat. 'White men been sweatin' their guts out for a spoonful of gold dust, and these goddamn wetbacks come apourin' in — and find a bonanza! Din' sit right with me. Got a few boys together an' we took it off 'em.'

'You took it.' At Satterlee's wary glance, Bannerman added, 'You were the only survivor, weren't you? You left Benedict for dead. Tim Willard was already dead and so were the rest of your bunch. Must've been mighty profitable for you.'

Satterlee shrugged.

'What'd you do with all that gold, that you took this job offered by Mariah? Two thousand dollars isn't much incentive.'

'Well, I damn well din' save it in no

coffee can, sittin' there doin' no good. I *spent* it, you dumb Reb!'

'Lot to get through in a short time.'

'Hell. More where it come from. This deal sounds like it might work out well. More than the two thousand.'

Bannerman hitched around, straightening, drawing on his cheroot, his eyes steady on Satterlee.

'Got a hunch you knew about this so-called 'bonus' before she told us.'

'You follow hunches?'

'Sometimes. You know more about this deal than the rest of us?'

'Whatever I know, I'm keepin' to myself.' Satterlee looked hard at Bannerman. 'But I'll say this: it could pay very good — if the woman didn't exaggerate, and I figure she got the right info. She spread her money in the right places.'

'And a few words got back to you.'

Satterlee shrugged, returning the gaze. 'I go for as big a share as I can get . . . Any way I can do it.'

He flicked his half-smoked cigarette

away and hitched at his gun-belt.

'Always best when you stick close to a good plan, Wiley. According to Mariah, anyway.'

'Mmmm . . . Me, I like to play it by ear. Always been a loner.'

'Me, too. Likely why when I find a good friend, I stand by him.'

Wiley Satterlee's eyes slid around. 'We still talkin' about Benedict?'

'I regard him as a good friend. Worked with him three, four times. Stuck his neck out for my sister once and saved us all a helluva lot of trouble.'

'Ah, yeah. You're one of them fellers; figure you owe someone and just can't rest easy till you square away.'

'That's me.'

'All them Mexes were with that mule train are dead. I took care of 'em. Nothin' to square for Benedict now.'

'If that's right, there's nothing. But Todd thinks he recollects ridin' out of the pass, with you still shooting — behind him.'

Satterlee looked genuinely surprised.

'Yeah? Aw, one of my bullets din' ricochet an' hit him in the back, did it? I mean, that what he thinks? Hell almighty, that never even ocurred to me. He just rode on out an' kept ridin'. I yelled after him three, four times, but he kept goin'.' He looked levelly at Bannerman now. 'And he din' come back, which, in my book, gives me the right to the pickin's.'

'You must've seen he was hit — and you never went after him to see if you could help.'

'Well, looked to me like he was about done for and there'd been a lot of shootin' an' I was knee-deep in dead men. You wouldn't've hung around, would you?'

'Not if I was you, no.'

Satterlee scrubbed a hand around his jaw. 'Mebbe I could take that further, but reckon I'll let it go . . . for now. We gotta work together on this. If there's anything you figure needs to be squared, why we can talk it over afterwards. OK?'

'I'm all through talking, Wiley.'

Satterlee's eyes narrowed as he straightened quickly. He dropped his gaze to Bannerman's gun but the man hadn't made any kind of a move towards the weapon.

'Mariah'll be kinda upset we go head to head.'

'I'll wait. I can use the money for one thing. But you know how it is between us now.'

Wiley shrugged unconcernedly. 'Hey, I could use one of them cheroots. They smell fine.'

'Two bits a packet at any store,' Bannerman told him shortly. He flicked away the half-smoked cheroot as he stepped out into the sunshine, away from the shade of the dogrun, and ground it into the dust.

Satterlee stayed put, mouth tight, eyes pinched, his coarse face set in thoughtful lines. There was no trace of fear as he watched Bannerman stroll away. None at all.

Bannerman was drinking from the tin

dipper on a chain at the well when Mariah came out from one of the bunkhouses.

'You had a long talk with Satterlee, I see.'

He wiped the back of his wrist across his mouth, hung the dipper up. 'Few things we needed to say to each other.'

'You knew I'd hired him, didn't you? Even before you were approached by my agent. I can see there's something between you. Maybe it's even why you took the job.' When he said nothing, she added, 'I heard you're a man likes to be paid up front. Yet this time . . . '

'An exception. Maybe I like your style.'

She straightened. 'And maybe you just like being close to Satterlee because of something that happened between you.'

'Never met him before today.'

She studied his face closely, nodded very briefly. 'Just do what you're being paid for, that's all.'

'I always give value for money.'

'You better. You *all* better.'

And he knew that there was something mighty important to her attached to this job.

Mighty important.

4

First Round

It was Tony Ramirez who warned him.

This was the third day on Crown and Mariah had still worked, with Dakota, to keep the six hired guns separate from her crew. The latter were naturally curious, and possibly even recognized one or two of the gunfighters. But going by the way they hurried about their chores when Dakota showed, toting his rifle and his usual mean look, they had learned from the past not to force their curiosity.

Bannerman was having a pre-supper cheroot under the elm near the biggest of the yard wells when the Mexican appeared, lifting the dipper and sipping from the brimming cup. He glanced across at Bannerman who nodded.

'Long way from Juárez and his

rebeldes, eh, amigo?'

'Yeah. They were wild times, Tony. Thought you'd be married off to that *señorita* by now. What was her name . . . ? Rosa . . . ?'

'Rosalita. Ah, well. She had a younger sister, Evangelina, and . . . ' He shrugged, giving Bannerman a glimpse of that boyish smile. 'I could not have sisters fighting over me, breaking up a nice family, could I? So I did not marry either. Instead, I found it . . . wise to ride north to the Rio and look for work in this fine country of yours.'

Bannerman smiled. 'Yeah! I bet you haven't noticed much of the country — just some of the folk who live in it. Of the feminine gender, I'd say.'

Tony made a wide gesture with his womanish hands. 'We-ell. Perhaps that is why I have travelled so far north. I find the air much . . . healthier up here. But, ah, the memories.'

'Tony, you'll be lucky if you grow old enough to enjoy 'em, you don't stay away from the women. Someone'll slip

72

a blade between your ribs, one of these times when you least expect it.'

He was surprised to find Ramirez's face was very sober now. 'Heath, speaking of blades, I came across Satterlee honing a slim blade yesterday. He did not see me. But I saw him — slipping the blade back into a sheath he keeps — here.'

He reached up and touched the back of his shirt collar.

'If things go badly for him in a fight . . . ' The Mexican shrugged. 'Just be careful, amigo. I think maybe he will not wait until after this *trabajo* to settle your difficulties.'

'Thanks, Tony. Our trouble's that obvious, eh?'

'*Sí*. There are some who wish it would flare up and one of you kill the other. Then there will be a bigger share for the rest of us.'

Bannerman smiled crookedly. 'I'd like to meet the feller who said 'Honour among thieves . . . ' He must've been reading the Brothers Grimm.'

'Of course. But be warned, Heath. Wiley Satterlee is a greedy and ruthless *hombre*.'

★ ★ ★

The increasing hostility between Bannerman and Satterlee must have been noticeable to Mariah, too — and it bothered her. She couldn't afford dissension amongst her hired guns; she needed them all to ensure the success of her venture.

So while they were eating supper she appeared, with Dakota and seven heavily armed ranch hands, who looked tough though nervous, having been called upon to hold their weapons on these hired gunfighters.

The men at the table stopped with their mouths full of half-chewed food or forks midway to their faces; one, Caldwell, freezing as he reached for a bottle of sauce.

Seven shotguns covered them, and Dakota's rifle for good measure. The woman stared at them bleakly.

'I'm taking your guns.'

Her words, said flatly, no argument, brought frowns and a couple of curses, but these professionals knew not to take any chances with nervous men holding cocked and deadly weapons.

'I'm sorry. But I can see that not all of you get along as well you might.' Her eyes slid across Bannerman and Satterlee, sitting opposite each other. 'I can't afford to have you fighting among yourselves, maybe maiming or killing each other. I need you all. So we're going to confiscate your weapons and lock them in the ranch safe until we're ready to proceed with the job.'

None of them was wearing guns at the table and without turning, she spoke to two of the ranch hands, told them to go into the section allotted to the gunfighters for living-quarters and collect the handguns and rifles.

'You ain't takin' my guns,' growled Wiley Satterlee, and Kid Shipley added his displeasure, but the two men hurried off and Mariah's determination didn't waver.

'It's best in the long run. You won't need your guns here on Crown. If you must . . . cross swords with each other over something, then put a hold on your hostilities until after we do this chore. Carry on with your meal, gentlemen.' She began to turn away, then swung back. 'Oh, by the way, don't approach the main house closer than about ten yards from now on, night or day. There will be armed guards watching. This does not apply to you, Mr Flood. If you have any queries or can show me a projected plan, you may approach. Just do it carefully and make sure you come in adequate light so you can be recognized.'

'This is gonna cost you, lady!' growled Caldwell. 'I want at least five thousand dollars, now — *at least*! And you better be willin' to guarantee it.'

Several of the others backed him. Mariah hesitated, then nodded jerkily. 'Very well. If there isn't enough in the train's safe to give each of you five thousand dollars, then I will guarantee to make up the difference.'

The men came back and reported the guns were ready to be locked in the ranch's big safe. Then Dakota and the ranch hands backed off into the gathering dusk.

'You two caused this!' growled Kid Shipley, glaring at Bannerman and Satterlee.

'What the hell,' murmured Satterlee. 'She's right — we won't need our guns here.' He looked squarely across the table at Bannerman. 'Any differences we got can wait — right?'

Bannerman nodded shortly, reaching for another beefsteak with his fork. 'They'll still be there after the chore, Wiley, and for a long time after that. Until they're squared away.'

Their eyes locked briefly, then they continued eating, but there was a lot of hostile discussion about the woman's move.

Bannerman saddled his roan after smoking his usual cheroot and rode off into the fading light, towards the hills.

There was a gleam of a vast lake or something up there; he had seen it the last two nights, just on sundown, the light catching it at that time. But he couldn't find it on the big wall map and he didn't ask, he was just naturally secretive about where he rode.

And now he was without his six-gun or rifle as security.

It was almost night; some stars were twinkling over a low range in the north east when he topped out on a ridge and found the answer. It wasn't a lake, it was a vast dam. Or a series of three dams, interlocking, covering many acres. Looking carefully as it gradually grew darker, he saw the run-off channels and a raised wooden-sided flume, dog-legging for miles down through the small hillocks, branching several times. He couldn't see them now, but he knew by the map that there were several smaller ranches out in that basin and, beyond, the town itself.

'By God!' he said, half-aloud. 'This supplies water to most of the basin and the damn town as well.'

And it was all on Crown's land! He whistled softly. No wonder Mariah Birdwood was treated with so much respect; she virtually controlled the water supply for more than a thousand people: farms, homes, ranches, businesses. Now that was real power; better than money if ever she was ruthless enough to take advantage of it.

'*Give me what I want, or I close the headgates* . . . .' That's all it would take.

Of course, it wasn't likely it would — or even could — come to that. There were bound to be legal safeguards in place so that such a situation would never arise. Which still didn't mean it *couldn't* happen.

Many times, guns had been known to take precedence over any scrap of paper with fancy copperplate writing and a few wax seals.

* * *

He sat on a rock while his horse browsed on some grass and took out his cheroots. As the match flared, out of the corner of his eye he saw movement — not clearly, but fast and coming towards him.

Instinct rolled him off the rock in a flash and, as he landed on his knees, his right hand automatically went to his hip; but, of course, there was no gun.

Then the shape was hurtling towards him: a big body with a punched-in hat and reaching hands, one of which held a broken tree-root about three inches thick. It whistled and thudded on to the rock, sending splinters and dust flying.

Wiley Satterlee grunted, spat an expletive, and tossed the remnants of the shattered club aside. He dived over the rock and collided with Bannerman as he started to rise.

They crashed to the ground, both grappling for a hold, using each other for support. Satterlee bared his teeth and hooked an elbow alongside Bannerman's jaw, which knocked the man sideways. Satterlee kicked his legs from under him and, as Bannerman hit, sprawling, Wiley raised a boot and stomped at his head. Bannerman rolled away. The boot caught his shirt and tore the cloth, raked some flesh from his shoulder. It seared in a flash of pain that drove Bannerman into a spinning roll, clutching at tufts of grass to slow his momentum and twist around as Wiley charged in. He raked his boot heels across Satterlee's shins and the man howled, stopped, then leapt in an impromptu dance of agony.

Bannerman came up to his feet, got his boots planted firmly on the angle of the slope and slammed two wide-looping blows into the other's midriff. Satterlee staggered and one leg gave way. Bannerman planted a knee into his face, sending the man's hat rolling. He twisted fingers in Wiley's long hair, yanked his head hard to one side, wrenching the neck muscles painfully.

Wiley grunted and came lunging up, the top of his head almost catching Bannerman under the jaw. Bannerman jerked his head back in time but the edge of his jawbone took some of the passing force. His teeth clacked together audibly and he tasted blood. Satterlee locked his hands around the gunfighter's neck and squeezed, his eyes bulging in mad fury.

Instinctively, Bannerman grabbed the tendon-taut hands, gripped one little finger and forced it back, twisting until it was about to snap. Satterlee let go with a yell and Bannerman's throat burned as air roared into his lungs. The rush made him dizzy and he faltered. Wiley Satterlee hit him in the midriff, tried an uppercut, but Bannerman managed to get his head out of the way, then snapped it forward and saw stars as his forehead crushed Satterlee's nose.

Hot blood spurted into his face as the cartilage crunched and Satterlee went down to one knee. Bannerman clubbed him on the side of the head, using his fist like a hammer, and Wiley rolled, slid downslope. As he whipped to his knees, his right hand went to the back of his neck. Bannerman, starting to rush forward, threw himself to one side, diving groundward.

Light streaked from honed steel and he heard the soft whistle as the thrown blade passed overhead. It clattered against a boulder behind him. Then Satterlee was coming at him with a fist-sized rock raised, ready to smash his skull.

There was no doubt now this was to be a fight to the death; maybe Satterlee had notions of dumping his body in the deepwater dam, the roan, too, and no one would ever know for sure what had happened to Heath Bannerman. Just went riding in the dusk and never came back . . .

The rock swung down but Bannerman was no longer there. He rolled on to his back and swung up his legs, both boots rising as he snapped his limbs straight. The worn high heels took Satterlee in the midriff, just under the arch of the ribs. The man gave a strangled scream, lifted to his toes and toppled sideways. He rolled down against Bannerman who kicked free, spun on top of the man, driving a knee into his belly. He took Wiley's big ears in his hands and hammered the man's head into the ground several times. Satterlee went limp and lay there, breathing noisily as blood bubbled out of his squashed nose. He coughed a few times, hawking reflexively.

Bannerman propped himself on one elbow, dragging down great lungfuls of air, his head spinning, feeling the growing aches and pains from his injuries. He sat back against the rock that the thrown blade had struck, and held the knife in front of Wiley's pain-filled eyes as the man, semiconscious, fought to steady his breathing.

'You must — be — slowing down — Wiley. To have to — de — depend on a — hideaway like — this . . . '

Satterlee glared, reached feebly for the blade. Bannerman pulled it out of reach easily. He slashed once, a downward stroke, and the damaged tip ripped a gash in Satterlee's left cheek, from under his eye to the jawbone: a mark for life. Wiley gasped and clapped a hand against the wound, blood oozing through his fingers.

'Just a reminder this ain't finished.' Bannerman stood and hurled the blade as far as he could into the darkening waters of the damn. The *plop* was audible even above the whine of gathering insects.

'S — son — uver!' Satterlee growled. 'You're dead!'

'One of us will be — and sometime soon.' Heath gestured to the spreading ripples on the dam.

Satterlee went very still, except for

his heaving chest. Then he shook his head, smiling crookedly through the blood. 'Nah — not you. You don't kill — that way.'

'I could make an exception.'

'Uh-uh. You like a — a square off. Damn fool! I'll get you, anytime, any way I can . . . ' His hand was dripping blood now.

'Yeah. Todd warned me you would. And I know it. Any man who'd shoot another in the back, one who'd just sided him, would pull that kinda lousy deal.'

'Benedict says I shot him in the back? That your beef with me?'

'You shot him, all right. So you'd have all that Mex gold to yourself.'

Satterlee shrugged, but winced; he had collected some body damage, too. 'Mebbe you better — grow eyes in the — back of your head.'

'Wish I could. But I'll be ready now. You'll go through with the job — and mebbe try for me as soon as it's done. But I'll be watching, Wiley. And you'll see it coming, I promise you.'

Satterlee fought to undo his neckerchief and held it against his bleeding face.

'Benedict sure must've done plenty for you.'

Bannerman said nothing and Satterlee tried to struggle up. The gunfighter stood over him, placed a boot in his side and thrust violently. Satterlee rolled over, down the slope and splashed into the mud at the edge of the water.

While he floundered, spitting gobbets of mud, half-choked, Bannerman staggered up to his waiting roan, mounted and rode off, silhouetted against the now star-spread sky until he dropped from sight below the ridge.

Satterlee's mount came towards him from behind a clump of rocks, looking for company. He leaned from the saddle and grabbed the dangling reins; Satterlee had obviously just left it to graze while he sought out Bannerman.

Now Bannerman rode on, leading

Satterlee's mount, down the slope to the edge of the Laramie Plains.

A long walk back would maybe cool Satterlee down.

Or make him kill-crazy.

Right now, Bannerman didn't care which.

5

Plans

Jonas Flood had a curtained-off section at the rear of the living-quarters, away from the main sleeping and lounging area, where he could work on his plans for the train robbery.

No use calling it anything else: hold-up, stopping, flagging it down. It was a robbery. And men were going to die and money — and something as yet unnamed — would be stolen. It was all familiar ground to Flood.

'When does the train run?' he had asked Mariah and she had told him: within ten days or two weeks.

'I can't be more exact. I need to wait for my . . . contact to give me the timetable.' Her gaze sharpened. 'I heard you're very good, Mr Flood, good and . . . fast.'

He nodded, scratching lightly at his widow's peak on his sweating brow. 'Two weeks is plenty of time, even ten days. But I need to know the route.'

'Surely that's already clear. It will follow the tracks. It has to.'

He looked at her steadily. 'How many sets of switch points are between the start and the Laramie Plains? Each one leads to a siding or a side-track. Each could set it off in a different direction. Or the special car could be hitched to another train that's waiting. That's why I need a better map.'

'The one you're using is up to date.'

'I didn't say a more recent map, I said a *better* one. A *railroad* map, showing all the points and side-tracks. Can you get one?'

She was frowning now and her mouth had tightened in her annoyance. 'I can try, but there'll be some delay in getting it up here. You should have mentioned it earlier.'

'I got no gypsy in me, Miz Birdwood, and I don't know where I could lay my hands on a crystal ball. So, seeing as I didn't even know why you were hiring me — '

Irritably, she held up a hand. 'All right! I'll have to send a man into town in the morning and see what can be arranged. Can you get on with anything while I do that?'

'Basic stuff. All will depend on the best place for the hold-up. But I can work out things in general.' He smiled thinly. 'I'm familiar with several kinds of railroad express cars and their layouts. They don't differ much.'

She was about to speak when the curtain was pushed aside and Dakota stood there, rifle in hand. He looked tense.

'Can you come?'

Her frown deepened. 'Right now?'

He nodded. 'Somethin' you should see.'

She swore softly under her breath and nodded jerkily to Flood. She followed Dakota through the curtain and down the long hut where the others were lounging, playing desultory poker for vestas.

She felt their hard eyes on her as she followed Dakota out into the night.

'What is it?' she snapped. He gestured towards the corrals where a man was off-saddling two horses. She squinted and recognized Heath Bannerman. She turned her gaze quizzically to Dakota.

'Just rode in, forking his roan, leadin' the other. It's Satterlee's mount.'

She stiffened. 'And . . . Satterlee?'

Dakota shook his head. 'No sign.'

'Bring your rifle!'

Bannerman was just hanging Wiley Satterlee's saddle over the top corral rail when they came hurrying up. A wash of light from under the dogrun, outside the open bunkhouse door, showed his battered face before he could tug down the brim of his hat any lower.

'What the hell have you done with him?' she demanded.

'Who?'

'Don't play dumb with me, Bannerman! Look at you! Bruised and swollen, knuckles split! You've been brawling — and it has to've been with Satterlee.'

He nodded. 'He jumped me up by that big dam.'

Her face sharpened. 'You're not supposed to go up there! It's right on our boundary. You've been told to stay close to the house.'

'We had a bit of a brawl,' he said, ignoring the censure. 'First round in a fight that's coming up between us.'

'I told you — and I told Satterlee — that there was to be none of that until after the job! You gave me your word!'

'And I stuck by it. Thing is, Wiley's word never did mean a damn thing.'

Her breasts were heaving. She glared at him and said in a voice of forced calm, 'Is he . . . all right?'

'Yeah. Might need a sawbones.'

'Good God! What . . . did you do to him?'

'He tried to use a knife on me. I put

my mark on him — with the blade. Might need stitching.' He touched his cheek.

She looked sharply at the silent Dakota. 'Wouldn't've minded seein' that,' the Indian allowed. 'You're both big men. Lucky at least one of you wasn't crippled.'

'You can ride into town with Satterlee when he shows up, then,' Mariah snapped. 'And he can give you a blow-by-blow description.'

Dakota shrugged; he was used to her moodiness.

'I take it, Wiley *will* show up?' she snapped at Bannerman.

'He's afoot, so maybe it'll take him some time. You through with me? I'd like to wash up and grab some shut-eye.'

Annoyed still, she gestured sharply to the wash benches beside the bunk-houses. 'And you stay away from Satterlee when he comes. Dakota, you see to it. Meanwhile I'll write you a note I want you to take to Sheriff

Magraw. Tell him he's to give it to the land agent, even if he has to drag him out of bed. And he's to wait and give you what I'm requesting. You bring it back here and give it to me, no matter how late. And make sure Satterlee comes with you. You understand?'

'Whatever you say.' Dakota lowered the rifle as Bannerman walked towards the wash benches, limping slightly. 'Hope I'm around afterwards to see them two square away,' he said.

But Mariah was already striding back to the main house, her shoulders set in rigid lines. Dakota knew why: she always — *always* — had to be obeyed, to the letter.

He had learned it a long time ago; it was the only way to get along with Mariah Birdwood.

★   ★   ★

She couldn't believe it.

The crew had already eaten their breakfast and were moving about, preparing for their daily chores. The gunfighters were sitting at their far end of the long table under the dogrun, most still eating, one or two lighting smokes. Satterlee sat at a distance from the others, a plaster on his face covering the cut and the seven stitches the doctor had used to sew his cheek.

He chomped determinedly at his food, his face bruised and swollen, just as Bannerman's was. He glared steadily and murderously at Bannerman all the time.

She would have to keep a close eye on those two.

But, even as she thought it, on her way to see Flood and take him the railroad map Dakota had brought back from town last night, Bannerman got up from the stool at the table and walked directly to the corrals. He took down a riato from a post, ducked between the bars and singled out his roan.

In minutes he had it roped and was throwing his saddle on its back.

Face grim she hurried down as he tightened the cinchstrap, tested it, adjusted it a little, apparently oblivious of her approach.

'What d'you think you're doing?'

He turned and she saw, close up, that his jaw was swollen and bruised, there was a cut under his lower lip, and his left eye was half-closed under a lid and the socket was painted with rainbow hues.

'Lost my cheroot case. Must've fallen when Wiley and me were fighting.'

'I said you weren't to go up to the dam.'

His gaze was steady. 'You did. But I want that case.'

'I'll send Dakota to look around — '

'No need.' He swung a little stiffly into the saddle, settled with a couple of grimaces as sore muscles were used. 'Won't be long.'

She grabbed the roan's bridle, looking up at him coldly. 'I'm paying you. I expect you to obey me.'

'You've only paid me in part. I've got to get my main money the hard way.'

He wrenched the roan's head around and she had to step back hurriedly. By the time she had regained her balance, he was spurring out of the yard.

Mariah looked around for Dakota, cursing the man silently; he would still be sleeping, after his late ride last night.

She strode across to where the ranch crew, having watched the small drama, had paused in their preparations.

She took out her frustration on them, bawling them out angrily as lazy no-goods, haranguing them about her dissatisfaction with their work — imagined or otherwise.

And all the time she was getting angrier and angrier with herself, for giving way to such a childish display.

By now Bannerman was riding into the foothills and would soon be lost in the deep shadows.

★   ★   ★

On the slope above the dam, where the trampled ground showed the area he had fought over, Bannerman spent twenty minutes searching before he located his battered cheroot case. It was jammed down between two rocks, the leather scuffed and scratched, one of the silver-edged corners bent and twisted out of shape, likely ready to break off its anchoring point. The cheroots were a trifle flattened but still smokable and he lit one, sat on the rock and smoked it while he tried to clean up the case.

It had belonged to an old Mexican he had found abandoned and with two bullets in him, not far from one of Juárez's raids on a government supply train. The Mexican had been fighting on the side of the *rurales* but he told how he had been dragged from his family, given an old musket and a rust-spotted sabre and told to fight to the death — for Maximilian.

Bannerman had taken the old man to a ruined adobe shepherd's hut and doctored his wounds. Bannerman himself had a bullet in his side and after he had dug it out and cauterized the wound, needed rest before heading back across the Rio. The old man had recovered sufficiently to make it back to his family and in gratitude had given Bannerman the cheroot case, his only possession and one he prized greatly. It had originally come from Castille with one of his ancestors. Bannerman didn't want to take it but saw it was important to the old man that he repay his saviour . . .

It had been a fine case then, hand-tooled Cordoban leather, the silver chased and engraved with curling vines, one including a tiny humming bird and a flower . . .

Of course, it had to be that corner that was bent out of shape and in danger of coming loose now. But he buffed the leather as well as he could and stood up, to put it in his saddle-bag.

That was when he saw the rider up the slope, sitting a pinto with two upright black ears, a rifle casually pointing at him.

It was a girl in her early twenties; wheat-coloured hair spilled from beneath her small, neat hat, which was held on by a tie-thong with a silver slide under her small jaw. Even from here he could see how blue her eyes were, the way her small nose turned up slightly, the soft mouth — though it was a little tense now. She wore a faded range shirt and trousers.

'Who're you?'

Her voice was quiet, firm, and he saw she had one slim thumb resting on the ear of the rifle's hammer.

'Name's Heath Bannerman. Who might you be?'

She frowned slightly, shaking her head briefly to move a strand of golden hair the breeze had blown across her face. 'I'd think you are one of Mariah's gunfighters whom I've been hearing about — except you're not wearing a gun.'

'So you don't need to hold yours on me.'

She smiled a little. 'Making you nervous, am I? Well, Mr Bannerman, just because you appear to be unarmed doesn't necessarily make you less dangerous.'

He spread his hands, smiling, too. 'I'm not dangerous.'

She leaned forward slightly, studying his battered face. 'Have you had a fall?'

'Several. Nothing serious.' He held up the cheroot case. 'Dropped this up here last night. Came looking. Aren't you on Crown land here?'

The girl sobered. 'That's a matter . . . still to be decided.' Her face was sober now, the mouth a firm line. She studied him for another long moment, then put up the rifle, though she did not slide it into the scabbard under her left leg. 'I'm Lola Stanton.' She gestured with her small chin over her right shoulder. 'Beyond that rise is my ranch, the Box S. I run it with my brother, Kyle.'

'Believe I saw it marked on the survey map. A lot smaller than Crown.'

'Every ranch for fifty miles around is very much smaller than Crown.' *Was there a trace of bitterness in that warm voice* . . . ? 'Always have been. The Birdwoods were first to settle up here, nudged their way on to Indian land and held it by force. The rest of us had to squeeze in where we could.'

Bannerman pursed his lips. 'I heard Darby Birdwood got along tolerably well with the Indians — might even have a 'breed son . . . '

She scoffed. 'No doubt Mariah told you that — or some of her men did. It's a fantasy. Darby Birdwood had a lot of dealings with the Sioux and it's possible there is someone with his blood in their veins, but Indians will only take so much from a white man, and I mean so much in the way of 'gifts', like guns in exchange for putting an X on a piece of paper, 'giving' him many acres of their own land. They're not fools, you know. They take what they can, then, when they have had enough, they put a stop to it.'

'With those guns you mentioned? Or maybe the good old traditional bow and arrow . . . ?'

Lola Stanton's face was sober, then she smiled. 'I see you have had dealings with Indians, too, Mr Bannerman.'

'Comanche and some Apache. Different from the Sioux, but still know where their roots are. You're saying Birdwood built Crown on land he stole from the Sioux by coercion and a few old guns? I mean, it wouldn't be the first time Indians have been gypped that way but . . . '

She shrugged. 'Whether that's what happened or not, no one seems to care now. The government boundaries have changed and they skirt Crown, although in parts they cut across our ranch land; my father and our neighbours have lost out because of it.'

Bannerman said nothing. She straightened in the saddle and gestured towards the dam.

'What d'you think of our inland sea?'

'Good description. Box S own any

part of it? I can see there are three separate dams and — '

She shook her head sharply. 'No! The catchment area is almost completely on Crown's land. It segments down the bottom. Three small hills cleave the main run-off channel. It was easier, and no doubt cheaper, to combine the three in the big catchment on Crown. Washington paid us a pittance for what would encroach on Box S and our neighbours on Slant H and Pothook — said it was 'in the best interests of the Basin'.'

'And gave Crown control of the entire water supply?'

Her smile was crooked, knowing. 'I think Darby worked so hard to lobby for that that he almost destroyed his health. There was some Indian land incorporated, properly compensated for by Washington, but part was sacred land, a burial ground for their elders and ancestors. It's hinted that Darby inadvertently flooded it . . . '

Bannerman nodded. 'Now I see why Darby was shot full of arrows.'

Lola looked grim. 'There was a massacre in retaliation. Switchback Canyon on the Spade River. Heard about it?'

He shook his head.

'No. It was hushed up. But that's what happened.'

'And you and your Slant H and Pothook spreads don't get along with Crown because of that?'

'It does us no good. Darby Birdwood was smart, had plenty of friends high up in the army, even in Congress. I suppose it affected our parents more than us, but — well, it grates, Mr Bannerman. When we see Mariah strutting about . . . ' She paused, dragging down a deep breath. 'You have a way of . . . leading a person on, Mr Bannerman! I — I don't usually tell complete strangers such personal business.'

'Name's Heath. Bannerman's a bit of a mouthful. Well, ma'am, I can sympathize with you. Friend of mine, mostly crippled now, ran up against a similar thing. No dams, but land-grabbing. I've been helping him out because — well, I owed him something, and we're hoping a few thousand I get for this chore will set things right so he gets back what's rightfully his. He won't see much of the money, it'll all go to the lawyer who reckons he can pull off the deal and retrieve his land.'

'And that's why you're here? Hired by Mariah?'

He shrugged.

'I haven't heard of you, Mr Ban — Heath. But I'm told Mariah has brought in half a dozen notorious gunfighters and — well, as you can imagine, all three of us small ranchers are quite worried.'

'You can relax. It's nothing to do with you. Leastways, it might have something to do with the dam or the land, but she hasn't brought in gunfighters to raid your places and kick you off, if that's what's bothering you.'

Her blue eyes studied his battered face.

'I — have your word on that?'

'Will you take it? I mean we've only

been talking for a few minutes . . . '

'Yes. I'll accept your word if you give it to me. I like to think I'm a reasonable judge of character, and I think you're basically a good man.'

'You got me blushing! Well, I give you my word, as far as I know, Mariah didn't hire us to harry you or your friends. And if that's what she aims to do, I won't be a part of it.'

'All right. Thank you.' She stood in the stirrups and he saw that her legs in the whipcord trousers were quite long and slim as she looked around her. 'I'd better move along off Crown land — or what Mariah *claims* belongs to Crown — before she sends some of her crew to escort me to my line.'

'I'll escort you to your line.'

She hesitated, then nodded. 'All right.'

'This slope used to belong to you?'

'Still belongs to the Stantons as far as we're concerned. But Washington claims it is part of the natural catchment and feeds a major part of the dam. And, as

Birdwood had the most money sunk into the project . . . ' She paused and shrugged expressively.

'Hard to argue with that, I guess.'

'Hard to accept, Heath. Look at the grass here. Darn near knee-high. We lost a lot of truly good graze when this was given to Darby Birdwood. But there seems to be nothing we can do. So . . . '

Forgetting his stiff muscles, he swung aboard the roan and rode up alongside her. She smiled, wheeled her mount and started back over the rise above the sun-glinting water.

He touched his heels to the roan and followed.

6

Theories

The three armed men were waiting when they rounded the tall boulder just over the crest.

The girl gasped and reined down her pinto abruptly, having to fight it a little as it protested. Bannerman hauled rein, too, immediately recognizing the men.

One was Dakota, with his ever-present rifle — now aimed casually at Bannerman. The second was a big, thick-bellied man with a hard look but a flabby face — Bannerman had heard him called Corso, a roughneck tophand on Crown. The third man was another range rider, Shak someone, and he had been berated by Mariah for drinking on the job. She had stopped his wages for a week. What had surprised Bannerman, and the other gunfighters, was that the hardcase took it so mildly. At least on the surface.

'See, Dak?' said Corso, gesturing to the girl. 'Told you he come up here to meet the Stanton bitch.'

'Your mouth is long overdue for a dose of cattle-dip, Corso,' Lola told him with a curled lip.

'Some dental work with a gun barrel would be better,' Bannerman commented and Corso sneered.

'You've left it too late, gunfighter! You're in a heap of trouble now.'

'Leave it,' Dakota snapped to Corso, not taking his eyes off Bannerman. 'Shak, take the girl far as her line.'

'Aw, am I gonna miss out on all the fun?'

'*I'm* escorting Miss Stanton to her line,' Bannerman said, challengingly and for the first time he saw a half-smile on Dakota's bitter mouth.

'That so? Well, Corso was right about one thing. You're in a lot of trouble. Mariah told you not to come up here, and you not only ignored her, you met with one of the folks she's got a quarrel with. Don't look good, Bannerman.'

'I don't care how it looks. I'm riding to the Box S line. Don't try to stop me, Dakota.'

'Hell, Dak, he ain't even wearin' a gun! We gotta take his sass?'

'Told you to shut up, Corso. I'm handling this.' Dakota flicked his rifle barrel. 'Climb on down, Bannerman. You gotta learn to do what you're told — the hard way.'

Lola reached out and placed a hand on Bannerman's arm, frowning warningly. 'Don't . . . get into this. I'll ride on home. Thanks for the offer, anyway, Heath.'

'*Climb down, goddamnit!*' roared Dakota impatiently. Corso and Shak grinned at each other; Dakota was riled now and Bannerman was going to pay the penalty for causing it.

Bannerman started to climb down from the roan, one leg almost over the animal's back, when he grunted, wincing, let his boot slide back towards the stirrup.

'Must've pulled a back muscle,' he gasped, seeing the concern on the girl's face.

Dakota frowned and Corso and Shak just sat there, grinning, waiting for events they had seen before with other men who had crossed Dakota.

But this time it was not quite the same. Bannerman settled and rammed his spurs home, startling the roan — and everyone else. The horse whickered with a wild toss of its head and lunged up the slope, covering the few yards to Dakota in seconds. Dakota tried to pull his mount aside but the roan crashed into him and both horses went down, hoofs slashing, legs tangling. Corso and Shak fought their own suddenly skittish mounts and Lola blinked as she pulled the pinto to one side.

Bannerman, stiff back or not, launched himself out of the mêlée, grappled for Dakota's long-barrelled rifle. The man tightened his grip, teeth bared and eyes wild and murderous as he realized that Bannerman had the advantage.

The gunfighter heaved up and then down, dropping a knee into Dakota's chest. The man's breath gusted out and his grip loosened.

In a flash, Bannerman had hold of the rifle and he slammed the butt across Dakota's head, knocking the man floundering. The horses fought to their feet and, snorting, lunged away. A six-gun crashed as Corso, startled, reacted instinctively, though belatedly, and drew his Colt, throwing down in a fast wild shot. Crouching, Bannerman triggered the rifle, levered in a second shot and put the barrel on Shak who was just sliding his Colt free of leather.

The rifle thundered again and Shak was hurled back over his horse's rump. He crashed, thrashing, to the ground.

Corso was down, nursing a shattered shoulder, all the fight gone out of him. Dakota was barely conscious, hat off, one side of his head already swelling. Bannerman straightened slowly and looked at the girl.

Her big blue eyes were bigger than

ever as she stared, stunned at the speed of the violence and its outcome.

'My! I — I've never seen anything like that!' she breathed, her face paler than before.

Bannerman watched the Crown men. Shak had a bullet graze along the left side of his head and sat up, dazed. Corso moaned, looked mighty sick.

Dakota struggled half-erect, shook his head and moaned, grabbing at it, as he set his murderous gaze on Bannerman.

'Mariah'll have your scalp for this!'

'More likely yours, for making a mess of things. Get up and off-saddle your mounts; there'll be cloth and things in the bags you can use to patch up these two. And you can even go down to the dam and soak your head if you want. In any case, you three are gonna be walking back.'

Dakota's lips drew back from his teeth, his lips were bloodless, his mouth thinned to a razor slash. He didn't say any more. He didn't have to. It was all there on his face:

He was going to kill Bannerman at the first opportunity.

Bannerman collected guns and the Crown men's horses, mounted the roan and gestured for the girl to lead the way.

★   ★   ★

When he arrived back at Crown, Mariah and several cowhands were waiting in the yard between the corrals and the smallest of the three barns. She strode forward, face bone-white, eyes glittering.

'I can't believe I made such a mistake in hiring you!'

She gestured and two of the men came forward, taking the reins of Dakota's, Corso's and Shak's mounts from Bannerman. He dismounted a little stiffly, and they stared at Dakota's long rifle in his hands. The gun rigs of the others dangled from the saddle horn.

'I found my cheroot case.'

Mariah's face tightened even more. 'To *hell* with your damn cheroot case! What've you done with Dakota and my men? Have you . . . killed them?'

'Not this time. Though I doubt they'll want to come after me again.' He tossed the rifle to another of the cowboys. 'It's empty: I jacked out all the shells. I dunno what Dakota had in mind — or what your orders to him were — but he's gonna be nursing a sore head for a day or two. Corso will likely need a doctor to dig the slug out of his shoulder, and Shak's got a head-crease that with a little luck likely won't make him any stupider than he already is.'

'I'm seriously thinking of firing you, Bannerman!'

'Better not. I know what you're about. Not all the details, but enough to throw a spanner in the works if I was so minded.'

She frowned, blinked at his words. 'Why? Why d'you do what I tell you not to?'

'Told you once, I'll follow orders if they make good sense. Your tantrums make no more sense than a schoolgirl's.'

'You are the most insolent man I've ever met.'

'I doubt it. It's just that I don't take to bullying, and just because someone owns a lot of land and has a heap of money, don't mean a thing to me.'

Her jaw muscles were working as she ground her teeth. 'Well, I'm honest enough to admit that any man who can turn the tables on Dakota is worth keeping on the payroll. But I won't have any more of this. So be warned.'

She had started to turn away when he said, 'Ran into a neighbour of yours up at the dam: Lola Stanton.'

Mariah spun, eyes widening. 'What was she doing on my land?'

'Never asked her. But she did say there's some dispute about whether the land belongs to Block S or Crown.'

'There's no damn dispute! It was settled long ago. The trouble is, people like the Stantons and their smalltime neighbours fail to realize that Wyoming is still a Territory, and therefore under Federal jurisdiction, which means Washington. Local decisions about land area and boundaries and so on don't mean a thing. Washington has the last say, and if they change them . . . ' She shrugged.

'Depends how they change them, I guess. Or how much influence some people have in Washington.'

Her fine body stiffened and her eyes narrowed. 'You're a stranger here; you know absolutely nothing about local politics or disputes. What's more, it's none of your business. You live here on Crown, at my expense, until it's time to do the job you were hired for. Nothing more. Do I make myself clear?'

He hesitated, then nodded. 'Think I savvy,' he said with maddening sarcasm. 'How're things coming along, anyway? Flood come up with a plan yet?'

'He said he may have a rough outline by tonight. So don't go taking any more sundown rides.' She turned away and

119

added, 'Whether it's just to see the country — or to meet Lola Stanton.'

He smiled thinly as she stomped back towards the house. The crew stood there awkwardly, holding the guns, not sure what to do. Bannerman ignored them and began to unsaddle the roan.

From a stool under the rear of the dogrun, Satterlee drew deeply on his cigarette, wincing as his stitched cheek was sucked against his teeth. He watched every move Bannerman made but when the gunfighter turned the roan into the corral and started back towards their living-quarters, Wiley Satterlee stood quickly and walked across to the cookhouse.

*   *   *

After supper, while everyone was still at the table, rolling cigarettes or packing pipes, Mariah Birdwood came in and looked at Jonas Flood.

'You're ready to give us your outline, Mr Flood?'

'I am, but you gotta remember, this is only a rough. I've just knocked it together from that railroad map you got for me. I haven't seen the actual country so there might have to be changes according to the landscape.'

'All right, gentlemen, gather round. Mr Flood has the floor.'

Flood wasn't embarrassed when all eyes turned to him as he pulled up a cardboard folder stuffed with papers that were covered in writing or sketches. He was quite at home outlining plans such as this and had earned himself something of a reputation for having had plenty of success in the past.

'Well, gents, there's a lot to be done all at the same time, but, as I say, it will depend on the country. I can read a map OK, was in the army for a spell as a surveyor, but this railroad map has concentrated on contours and landscape that would affect the laying of rail track. They may have ignored some of the bigger details that wouldn't bother them, such as a boulderfield — they'd simply skirt that if they had to; if not, they wouldn't even bother recording it on their maps. You savvy now what I mean?'

'I may be able to give you a description of the country if you need it,' Mariah said. 'I've ridden that railroad in many places. We've loaded cattle directly on to trains to save driving them into the Laramie stockyards.'

Flood acknowledged her offer, spread some of his papers, shuffled a handful until he found three pages that held sketches. 'We still can't be sure about the exact route . . . ' He arched his eyebrows quizzically at Mariah and she nodded.

'I'll have all details before we need to make any definite moves.'

'OK. Well, this is how I see it, after we've stopped the train — about here.' He poked a finger at a place on the map and the men drew closer for a better view. 'If they use another side track or shunt on to a siding for some reason,

122

we'll just have to adapt.'

'OK, OK,' growled Satterlee. 'Let's say the damn train's stopped, whether we do it or they stop of their own accord for some reason . . . '

Flood flicked him a cool glance and then returned to his sketch.

'I see the big problem as breaking into the express car,' spoke up Bannerman. 'Stopping a train's easy enough, but breaking open a special express car, full of armed guards, that's going to take a heap of doing.'

Jonas Flood drew down a deep breath, nodding impatiently. 'Yes — well, you're right, Bannerman, it won't be easy, but there is a way to do it.'

'Providin' we can get close enough,' said Kid Shipley. 'I've wrassled a few trains, but gettin' close to a car full of men shootin' to kill has helped turn my hair grey.' He touched the sprinkling of grey at his temples. Someone sniggered, but no one was in a mood for comedy.

'We do it from the roof,' Flood said, and when the noisy reaction died down, held up his hands. 'Yeah, I know, it's usually dangerous, but the railroad boys've outfoxed themselves this time. They've put a lining of armour plate on the underside of the roof, inside the car.'

'How in hell does that make it easier?' demanded Caldwell. 'Chris'sakes, we won't be able to even shoot through it!'

Flood smiled thinly. 'And they won't be able to shoot up through it, like they've done other times. The roof has always been dangerous because it's flimsy and bullets tear through it like paper. Which is why some bright railroad man had it lined with armour plate, so men up top can't shoot down through the roof into the car — and if the guards inside try to shoot up and nail any one on top, their own bullets'll kill them, flatten on the armour plate, ricochet back amongst 'em.'

There was a brief discussion and a few grins. Then someone asked the obvious:

'Then how the hell do we get through

the armour from topside?'

Flood smiled again. 'We don't. We rip off the cover of one of ventilators. Then we show them a bundle of dynamite with a burning fuse and tell them guards if they don't open the sliding door and let our men waiting beside the track into the car, they can have the dynamite — and share it among 'em.'

'Jeee-susss!' breathed Shipley.

Mariah smiled. 'Why, that's brilliant, Mr Flood!'

'Providing the guards don't start shooting at our men the moment the door's open and they jump out,' said Bannerman.

'No, Heath,' Flood said. 'We make sure they jam their guns through the loopholes first, *then* open the door and stay put with their hands in the air — '

Bannerman nodded slowly. 'Catch 'em between a rock and a hard place, eh? Get shot by us standing beside the track, or be blasted to hell from above if they try anything. You're doing well, Jonas. Now all we've got to do is open that special safe, which I'm betting will be made of armour plate as thick as the stuff on the ironclads in the War, like the *Merrimack* and *Monitor*.'

Flood was sober now. 'Yeah. It's gonna take a lot of dynamite, I figure; might even blow the car itself to matchwood and still leave the safe intact.'

All eyes turned to Mariah as she sucked in an audible breath.

'Gentlemen, I have some bad news. I have only a very limited supply of explosives. We've done a lot of tree-stumping and rock-blasting, smoothing out the catchment for the dam now that our wet season is imminent. I've only a few sticks left — I thought I'd be able to buy more in whatever quantity we needed. But there's talk of an Indian uprising and all sales of explosives are now on army permit only — a *detailed* permit, outlining intended use and so on. It has to be approved, and you know how fast the army moves on such things. We could be stymied right from the start!'

7

Ready –

'Steal it.'

All heads jerked up as Satterlee dropped the words into the throbbing silence left in the wake of Mariah's announcement. The silence dragged on into long moments, Satterlee sitting there, relaxed, big, scarred hands in his lap, looking smug beneath his bruises and cuts.

'We just go steal what we want. Anyone got a beef with that?'

'Steal it from where? A general store? They aren't allowed to keep much since those street riots when Waco Cassell's crew stampeded their herds through the town, then demolished much of what was left after they found the explosives bin in the store.' Mariah, mouth tight and bitter at the memory, shook her head swiftly. 'You'll need to come up with something better than that, Wiley.'

Satterlee shrugged and she added with annoyance:

'Don't even think of the fort. It may be only a few miles away but the powderhouse is under heavy guard night and day.'

Unperturbed, Satterlee smiled crookedly, making a hasty grab at his slashed cheek as he did so; the stiff facial muscles moved.

'Forget the damn army. There's a big mine back in the Bows, just took out a lease on a whole mountain back there. They're blastin' test pits and tunnels all over the countryside. Bet they got a whole damn powderhouse full of dynamite. All we gotta do is go collect it.'

There was another silence as the group digested this.

'How do you know this?' Mariah asked carefully. 'I haven't heard about any new mine.'

Satterlee smiled wider, ignoring the

pain in his cheek now. 'They're settin' up on the quiet because there's a chance the run-off from their process night reach your dam, or, at least the rivers and creeks.'

The woman was stiff now, eyes like stones, mouth thin and bloodless. 'What — kind — of run-off?'

'They're lookin' for copper, that's all I know.'

'And *how* do you know all this? I've already asked you once.'

'I was offered a chance to help hold up their first payroll. They're s'posed to be bringin' it in through the hills by mule train — helpin' to keep the mine operation quiet for a little longer.' He shrugged. 'Your offer was better, so I took it.'

'And I suppose that's an indication of how the rest of you feel, too! Money first — reasons afterwards.'

'If ever,' Bannerman told her flatly. 'What d'you think you've got here? A bunch of Sunday-school teachers? We make our living by our guns. Mostly it's all we've got to sell, so the highest bidder wins out every time.'

Her face was cold as she looked at him. She shifted her gaze to Satterlee after sweeping it around the men, who seemed to be in silent agreement with Bannerman's assessment of the situation.

'All right. After Wiley gives us some more details, layout of the buildings and the country and so on, we have to vote on this.'

Most of the men were for it already — anything that would mean they didn't have to go up against the army.

'Mr Bannerman?' Mariah said tightly. 'I don't believe we heard from you . . . You have some objections to the idea?'

'No. It sounds like a good one and likely the only way we'll get our hands on the dynamite we need.'

'But . . . ? You have a 'but', don't you?'

He nodded and Satterlee's eyes narrowed. 'Relax, Wiley. Good notion, like I said. If we can pull it off — *and keep it quiet*.' He waited for all the murmuring to die down. 'If it gets out that a couple of boxes of dynamite have been stolen, there'll be army patrols swarming over those mountains — and you can be sure they'll put even more guards on that train we're after. Just to be on the safe side.'

It took a few minutes for everyone to realize that Bannerman was right: the theft of a large amount of dynamite, from whatever source, was bound to arouse suspicion.

Mariah's small white teeth tugged at her bottom lip. 'It makes sense — but we need that explosive! Wiley, you'd better tell us all you know about this mine.'

'I was in on two plannin' sessions with the bunch that's gonna hit the mine's first pay train. They're takin' their time, 'cause it won't be for a few weeks. I did a stretch of watchin' for one whole day an' I can sketch the mine layout and the place where they keep the explosives. Won't be much trouble. Locked up tight, of course, but it's well away from the main buildin's and the bunkhouse. Those boys've got a real respect for dynamite.'

'Makes good sense,' Caldwell said soberly. The others stared and he held out his hands. 'See? Still ten fingers, both eyes and arms. Comes from bein' careful around explosives. And I aim to keep it that way.'

'All right. You're definitely one of the group who go in and get what we want,' Mariah said, mildly impatient. 'Is the powderhouse particularly strong, Wiley?'

'Dug into the hillside, likely lined with heavy logs — someone's done a heap of tree-fellin' around the area. The door's double-laid, maybe some metal down the inside, but that shouldn't worry us. There are three mighty big hasps and brass padlocks. Hefty screws or bolts from what I could see, but a pry bar should move 'em.'

'Pry bars have a bad habit of making the bolts screech as they draw them out of wood, amigo,' cautioned Tony Ramirez. 'I lost four good men one time

132

in Chihuahua when the sound woke the guard.'

'Take some oil and dribble it in on the shank as it comes out,' advised Kid Shipley.

'All right, we can work out the fine details later. As long as we're aware of what troubles we may meet we should be able to find ways to overcome them.'

'When do we do it?' asked Jonas Flood. 'I need to be sure I can work out the best way to hit the train. Incidentally, Mariah, we don't know its timetable yet.'

'I'll get it as soon as I can. I have to be careful how I go about showing an interest in such things.'

'Jonas, how about if we leave the dynamite till, say, the night before we hit the train?'

Bannerman was the centre of attention with his remark. Flood shook his head quickly.

'No good! Man, we can't even be sure we'd get our hands on the dynamite! And we'd have no chance of gettin' any more then. No, I have to know at least one full day — preferably two — ahead of time. I have to be certain sure we have all we need. It's no use on the day suddenly realizing we've forgotten something, with the train bearing down on us. Sorry, Bannerman.'

'Wait,' Mariah said. 'I think I see what Bannerman's getting at. If we steal the explosive too soon, the same thing will apply as if we try to rob the army powderhouse in the fort: there'll be a panic when it becomes known how much dynamite has been stolen and guards will be doubled on everything they think might be robbed.'

Flood sat back in his chair, mouth working in an almost inaudible curse. He flung his pencil on to his sketches. 'This is becoming more complicated by the minute!'

'It's why I'm paying you good money, Mr Flood! So you can plan around every eventuality we can think of.'

He nodded jerkily. 'Yeah, I know. It's just that it all seemed to be coming together so well — so easily. I might've known somethin' would jump up and kick me in the face.'

'There is another way, amigos,' said Tony Ramirez. When he had their full attention he added, 'We can steal the dynamite from the mine any time. *Sí*, I say any time!' He smiled slowly, showing very white teeth, spreading his womanish hands. 'All we have to do, after taking what we want, is to leave behind a stick of dynamite with a long fuse burning — in the powderhouse.'

He paused for effect, smile widening as he watched their puzzled faces.

'A long or slow-burning fuse will allow us to be a safe distance from the mine when the powderhouse explodes.'

'Christ!' someone exclaimed.

'What the hell use will that be?' demanded Satterlee. 'We'll have the whole shebang comin' after us, guns a'smokin'. Mebbe the damn mountain'll fall on us . . .'

His voice trailed off and a slow smile of comprehension spread across his battered features.

'Hey, wait up! You ain't as dumb as you look, greaser! Yeah! Blow the whole kit and caboodle — and they'll not only be chasin' their own tails, they'll never know if any dynamite's missin'! Just one big *boom*!' He threw up his arms, laughing now, ignoring the pain it caused his face. 'They'll wonder from now till Doomsday what happened, but they'll never know we stole our two cases of dynamite!'

Everyone saw now how it would work and the entire atmosphere of the special meeting lightened considerably.

They were under way with the big deal. This part was the *ready*, then would come *set*, and next, the final stage *go!*

★ ★ ★

Bannerman was surprised when Mariah came to the living quarters and asked him to come down to the corrals with her.

It was not yet noon and he had been

136

about to settle into a game of poker with a few of the others. At the corrals she turned and leaned against a fence post as he placed a boot on the lower rail beside her, took out his cheroot case — which he had repaired as well as he could manage — and lit up.

'I've just had word that a load of barbed wire has arrived in town. I want you to come with me while I pick it up.' Her gaze was cool. 'Normally, I'd take Dakota, but he's still having trouble with his balance and hearing. You'll have your guns, of course.'

'I wouldn't go without 'em,' he told her flatly, looking hard. 'How come you need an escort for barbed wire?'

'Just a precaution. It's been in short supply and I want to make sure I get what I need.'

So the storekeeper sends word all the way out here to let her know the wire's in — and whoever else needs some, will have to take what's left after Mariah Birdwood has had first pick.

Bannerman nodded to himself: *money!*

They rode out, trailing a buckboard driven by two rannies who had been working around the ranchyard. Just two regular ranch hands and a couple of rifles carelessly thrown in the back.

Bannerman himself had to admit he felt more 'whole' now that he was wearing his six-gun again and had his rifle in the saddle boot. Wouldn't surprise him if Satterlee and the others wanted their guns back now; he didn't aim to turn his in again. He thought maybe the girl already knew this might happen, but this trip to town was important enough to allow him to bring his guns.

There was more to this seemingly normal trip than met the eye, he decided.

He soon found out what it was when the buckboard pulled in behind the general store near the loading platform. There were already two other buckboards there and a small group of people seemed to be arguing on the raised landing.

He recognized Lola Stanton as one

and the young man beside her looked enough like her to have to be her brother Kyle. The other man on the fringe of the argument or whatever it was with the store owner was beefy, red-faced with large, calloused red hands: a typical sodbuster.

The storekeeper, Aaron Riddel, looked relieved when he recognized the Crown wagon.

'Ah, Mariah!' he called coming to the edge of the landing. 'I'm very pleased to see you. We seem to have a problem here with the distribution of the wire.'

Bannerman saw the high-stacked rolls of barbed wire against the walls of the store. He felt Lola Stanton's eyes upon him as he dismounted and looped the roan's reins loosely over the rail. He touched his hatbrim and she inclined her head a little, but seemed puzzled.

Riddel wiped his face with the edge of his apron. 'I — I've had to send for Sheriff Magraw, Mariah. I was hoping you would arrive earlier.' The way he looked at the Stantons and the sodbuster meant 'before the others', but he didn't say so. 'I haven't sold any wire yet — you have first choice, of course.'

'Oh, of course!' Lola Stanton spoke up quickly, surprising Bannerman some with the bitterness in those few small words. 'Crown must have special attention!'

Mariah's eyes flashed. 'I'm entitled to it. I spend ten times as much in this store as you and all the small ranchers and farms combined.'

'The way I heard it, you had no interest in this shipment of barbed wire, hadn't even bothered to order any!'

Mariah smiled. 'I've been very busy and I must've overlooked it. But Mr Riddel, courteous as always, was kind enough to inform me as soon as the shipment arrived, and to ask me if I would like some from the consignment, as he couldn't say when any more might be available.'

'Mighty thoughtful of him!' growled

the sodbuster, whose name was Madison. 'He won't sell us any until you've had your pick!'

Kyle Stanton, slightly younger than Lola, slim and good-looking, curled a lip. 'Yes. Very thoughtful of you, Aaron! It's not a very big shipment, but we need quite a lot to fence off our bottom land — '

'Kyle!' Lola snapped and the young brother stopped, flushed, realizing he had said more than he should have.

Mariah smiled slowly. 'So that's why you want the wire? And your land nudges right up against Box S, doesn't it Jesse? D'you really think fencing off will make any difference? I've claimed that land for Crown and I'll have the approval any time — '

'Nothin' to do with you, Mariah,' Madison growled. 'This is between Box S and me. We just aim to fence in some decent pasture before you decide to run one of your herds on to it, like you do on every other patch of grass you see.'

'But I am interested, as a matter of

fact, Jesse. And I'm very glad Aaron advised me about this shipment. I find I'm in need of a considerable quantity of barbed wire now. In fact, more than I see stacked against the wall.'

Bannerman felt the tension gripe him as he watched the others stiffen at Mariah's words.

'You — you aren't taking it all!' gasped Lola and Mariah's smile merely widened. 'Oh, you greedy bitch! You don't want barbed wire at all, do you? You just don't want me to have it. Or Jesse — or — anyone else!'

Mariah turned to her two cowboys. 'Start loading those rolls into the buckboard, Fletch. I'll settle with Mr Riddel and then we can get on back to Crown.'

'Damn you!' snapped the sodbuster. He snatched at the six-gun rammed into his belt, but froze when he saw Bannerman holding a cocked pistol on him. His big jaw sagged. 'H-How . . . Where the hell'd that come from?'

'Leave the gun, Jesse,' Bannerman

said. 'No call for that.'

'No call for you to be here neither!'

'I work for Crown, Jesse.' He spoke to the sodbuster but was looking at Lola and she knew he was also speaking to her. 'I've taken Crown money, and if I ride for the brand, I stick by it until I quit.'

'What noble principles you have, Mr Bannerman!' Lola said bitingly.

'Don't know no different, Lola.'

'I-I'm not sure whether that's something . . . worthy, or not. Right now, I mean.'

'It's the way it is. The way I am.'

'The hell's going on here?'

They all turned as Sheriff Pat Magraw came striding in. Riddel mopped his face again and said, 'About time, you showed up, Pat!'

Magraw ignored him, his narrowed gaze was on Bannerman now.

'You gonna put up that gun, mister?'

Magraw's Colt was half-drawn and Bannerman lowered his hammer, slid the weapon back into his holster. The lawman grunted but did not remove his hand from his own gun butt.

'Someone wanta to tell me what's happenin' here?'

'Hardly worth wasting our breath,' Lola Stanton replied coolly. 'We know you're on the Crown payroll, Pat, and any decision will be in their favour.'

'That so? Well, I like to think I'm a fair-minded man, Lola. S'pose you explain?'

It was Kyle who told the sheriff what was happening. 'She knows we ain't got the money to outbid her! She's gonna take all the damn wire and leave us none.'

'Well, I had thought of leaving half a dozen rolls for you and Jesse,' Mariah said without convincing anybody that she meant it.

'Hardly better than nothing,' Lola said, adding quickly, 'but we'll accept.'

Mariah shook her head. 'After your behaviour and attitude, I don't think I will leave any. I can always use an extra reel or two. Fletch, load the lot. Aaron, add it on to Crown's account.'

'Damn it! She don't even have to fork out any cash!' Jesse Madison said savagely. 'You don't run no monthly account with me, Aaron.'

'Well, you'll forgive me for sayin' so, Jesse, but you ain't as prosperous as Mariah. Her family's been customers at my store since I opened more'n twenty years ago.'

'Why'd you send for me?' the sheriff snapped at the storekeeper. 'There's no real trouble here. Unless this gunslinger aims to start any.'

Bannerman turned his gaze slowly to the sheriff. 'I'm not here to start trouble, Sheriff.'

Magraw snorted. 'Glad to hear you know better'n to try!' Bannerman looked away and said nothing. The arrogant sheriff mistook it for a back-down and couldn't resist strutting in front of his audience, small though it was. 'Yeah, you can be a big man out at Crown, but in my town, mister, you do what I say. An' you do it pronto.'

Bannerman's eyes lifted slowly. 'If I figure it's the thing to do.'

Magraw stiffened and he tilted his head back a little. 'You wanna push this? You like livin' dangerously?'

'I like living.'

Magraw smirked. 'Then just do what I tell you and you'll go on livin'. Get froggy, an' I'll tip you into an unmarked grave where you belong.'

'Pat! That's enough. Bannerman's only here to protect me and see we get the wire safely back to Crown.'

'Then tell him to keep his mouth shut or I'll shut it for him.'

'Like you did Big Casey's?' Bannerman asked tightly; that killing had stuck in his craw. Casey was just a big dumb friendly ox of a man, but this loud-mouthed lawman had to strut his stuff and show the town just how tough he could be: shooting a prisoner trying to escape — according to Magraw.

'Keep your nose outta my business, feller!'

'Don't think I will.'

'Bannerman!' Mariah's voice was sharp but he didn't look at her. 'Stop this! Stop it now!'

'Better get outta the line of fire, Mariah. I think Magraw's worked up enough guts to make a try for his gun!'

Riddel grabbed Mariah by the arm and pulled her back hurriedly. The others were already flattening against the wall as the two men faced each other, wondering how the situation had suddenly blown out to these dimensions.

Magraw knew he couldn't back down now; Bannerman knew it, too. The sheriff ran a tongue around his lips.

'Listen, gunfighter. You better think what you're doin'! You kill me — or even *try* to, an' you're in more trouble than you can shake a stick at!'

Bannerman smiled thinly and nodded, turning away. 'I thought so . . . '

'Watch out!' Later he figured it had been Lola Stanton who had shouted the warning, but at the sound of the words, he began his draw, twisting smoothly so

147

that he went down on one knee and the gun was in his right hand, blazing up at a slight angle, the bullet driving Magraw over the edge of the platform.

The sheriff lay still, face down in the dust and straw and dung.

8

Set –

Driving through the red dust of a Medicine Bow sundown, Mariah dropped back behind the laden buckboard and set her mount alongside Bannerman's.

'You prodded Magraw deliberately, didn't you? You wanted him to go for his gun.'

'That was his choice. I was turning away, remember?'

'You and your damn codes! Casey wasn't worth it.'

'Didn't reckon you'd think so. But I liked Casey. He knew he wasn't smart and that he had been used by almost everyone he'd come in contact with over the years, but he rolled with the punches, did his best — and he was loyal.'

'He also tried to punch your head off.'

'Because you told him to and he worked for you so he tried to do what you wanted.'

She frowned. 'Loyal, you said? The man stole my property.'

'Mebbe you better not push that line.'

She straightened quickly in the saddle. 'And just what does that mean?'

'I saw Casey's face when Magraw accused him. He didn't even know what Magraw was talking about. I'd guess he didn't eat too often up at your house to see any silverware lying about that might've interested him.'

She flushed, her mouth tight. 'He could've seen it any time. I sometimes have my meals on one of the balconies. He'd done chores in and around the house. He could've taken those salt- and pepper-shakers at any time . . . to spite me, because I'd fired him.'

'Why didn't you just let him go, instead of calling in a killer like Magraw?'

'You should be careful about who

you call 'killer', Bannerman!'

'Don't get off the subject. You sicked Magraw on to Casey for some reason — and Casey's dead.'

'So now you're blaming me?'

He gave her such a bleak look that she winced and felt a shiver pass through her entire body. 'You're just lucky you're not a man and packing a gun.'

'My God! You hardly knew Casey, yet you killed a lawman in a gunfight because of him.'

'Magraw had it coming. He'd lived too long. I've come across too many like him over the years, trading on folks' fears, just because he was big and mean.'

She half-hipped to look at him, painted red-gold now by the sun's rays. 'You trade on folks' fears of your guns.'

'Comes with the reputation, or I wouldn't have any reputation.'

After being silent a few moments she said, 'I suppose that's right. But you've made a bigger mistake than you know.'

He glanced at her briefly, not speaking, knowing she would tell him.

'You've just killed the man who was going to get us the information we need about the train's schedules.'

His head swivelled towards her. 'Magraw?'

'Yes! He was the sheriff! So he had to be notified about such trains going through his territory.'

'And he passed this info along to you? For money, I guess?'

'We had an arrangement, yes. Now that Pat's dead, I'm not sure what will happen.'

They rode in silence for a while, dropping off to one side in an effort to avoid some of the dust kicked up by the buckboard team.

'How soon were you expecting word to come through?'

'Any time now!' She was sharp with him, shaken by the killing of her man, and Bannerman's implication that he would have killed her, too, if she had been a man.

'Just keep it quiet — Magraw's death,

I mean. I guess it'll be all over town, but it don't have to get back to the railroad people before the train starts up this way, does it?'

'No-o. Provided it's not long in coming.' She was considering the suggestion. After some moments she nodded. 'We can try! But there's the railroad agent to consider. The information would be telegraphed to him, too.'

'Use a little more of your money. It seems to work wonders.'

She snapped her eyes at his curt suggestion. 'You're happy enough to take some of it!'

'I'm not beefing, Mariah. If you've already bought a piece of the agent, a little more to make sure he keeps quiet sounds like a good investment to me.'

When they topped out on a hogback rise, she turned to him and said flatly, 'You have altogether too much to say. You know that, Bannerman?'

He shrugged; it only made her madder and they rode the rest of the journey in silence.

She was met in the yard by the other gunfighters, all demanding the return of their weapons. She knew there was no way she could prevent them taking them if they really wanted to — especially now that Bannerman still had his six-gun and rifle.

'After supper then,' she relented, but anyone could see she was fuming underneath the unemotional face she allowed to show. She fixed her eyes on Satterlee. 'But there will be no trouble. It's too close to train time.'

She left it to Bannerman to tell them about Magraw but it was the ranch hands who had driven the buckboard loaded with barbed wire who told the story: Bannerman never mentioned it.

On the veranda after the meal Satterlee came out to stand beside Bannerman, adjusting his gun rig.

'Feel dressed now. So you got rid of the sheriff. Good idea.'

'Nothing to do with the train job.'

'You mean that Fletch was speakin' gospel when he said it was over that dimwit Casey?'

'It's done, Wiley. Leave it be.'

Satterlee was silent while he rolled a cigarette. 'Well, I heard you're a queer bird the way you look at things. Just don't ride off too damn fast, after the job, Bannerman, you and me have a coupla things to straighten out.' He grinned as he shook out his match, removed the cigarette from his puffy lips and blew smoke into Bannerman's face. 'Winner take all. You on?'

Bannerman turned. 'I might take you up on that.'

'OK by me. I'll be walkin' away rich.'

'One of us will.'

'*I* will.'

'Don't go spending it ahead of time, Wiley.'

Satterlee chuckled. 'Hell, I know exactly what I'm gonna do with my *dinero*. Had it planned ever since Mariah hired us. Only now I'll be able to do it *double*!'

It was sundown the next day when a rider came in fast from the direction of town. The gunfighters watched from their quarters as he skidded his mount in the yard, quit the saddle and sprinted towards the big house.

'Someone's in a hurry,' observed Josh Caldwell. 'I wonder if it's the word we been waitin' for?'

Nobody bothered answering but they were all tense and expectant when the man left a half-hour later. He sauntered back to his mount and had the look of someone who had just enjoyed a good meal.

'She's been entertainin' him!' Flood said, with a leer.

'Here she comes,' Satterlee whispered in his harsh voice, and they waited for Mariah to reach them.

It was obvious from her face that she was excited. 'The train has left Denver and will be at Fort Collins tomorrow. There are two more forts to call at before they cross into Wyoming, but they seem to be travelling fast, avoiding overnight stop-overs, so they'll reach Cheyenne on the morning of the eleventh, two days from now.'

'Hell, they're comin' faster than we figured!' Flood exclaimed. 'It doesn't give me much time. Is the route verified yet?'

'I have it in the ranch office; it's more or less as expected. Our railroad contact was very close in his estimation.'

''Very close' ain't good enough, Mariah. I've got to know exactly which line they're using and then work out where there are switch points they might use and — '

'That's what I'm paying you for, Jonas,' Mariah cut in sharply. 'You come up to the house with me and I'll go over things with you as I've been told. Quite a lot has been written down and there's a sketch of the route.'

Flood nodded, obviously tense, impatient to get started. He looked around at the others. 'Boys, looks like you'll be ridin' come daylight. You'll have to get that dynamite by tomorrow night.'

'We could save time by taking the dynamite direct to where we're gonna hit the train,' Kid Shipley said. 'You got a spot figured, Flood?'

'Tentatively. I chose the Lodgepole Creek crossing in the Laramie Mountains, but I'll have to make sure that the train will follow that route. I can do that as soon as I see Mariah's papers. And that's a good idea, Kid; takin' the dynamite straight there.'

'Hear that, boys?' spoke up Caldwell. 'We're all set!'

'Once we get the dynamite,' Bannerman reminded them. 'And nobody said that was gonna be easy.'

His words didn't even slow them down; the long wait was over. The blood was singing in the veins.

Now they could move.

9

Go!

There were many more lights at the mine than they had expected.

The hill where the buildings were situated reminded Bannerman of his childhood back in Arizona. Big Pig Hill they called it, because at one time the brush that had originally cloaked it had been swarming with razorback pigs, domestic animals that had escaped a Mormon wagon train years earlier and gone wild.

They had grown bolder as they bred and their numbers increased and they began coming into the town, robbing the garbage heaps, even chewing through wooden doors of root cellars where meat was hung and jars of preserves lined the shelves.

So a hunt had been organized. The

entire population of the town, except for the deacon and his family had set fire to the brush and, as the squealing boars and sows fled, they were picked off by every kind of firearm available.

The town glutted itself on pork for days until the flesh began to spoil. But the deacon, quick to get any kind of a religious message across to these heathens, demanded a gathering where the congregation could give thanks to the Lord for providing such a feast in these hard times.

He made it quite festive by asking everyone to bring either a lighted candle or a lantern and these were distributed across the slope and crest of the hill . . .

This mine layout was very similar and it took Bannerman and the others some time before they figured out why there were so many lights: they were marking the test pits, some of which were several feet deep, even having winding tunnels as the geologists followed likely-looking mineral-bearing veins of ore.

Where there had been a shaft sunk the top was marked by a square of red lanterns slung from a raised barrier of split logs. They had riddled the hill with the excavations but this wasn't the hill that interested the hired guns.

The one that contained the powder magazine was to the left and only three lanterns, set in a vertical line upslope, were burning. Crouched behind rocks, they watched men working the shafts, bringing out rubble in hand-barrows and tipping the tailings on to a spreading conical pile beneath a ledge cut into the earth. Only one shaft, larger than the lower ones, had a tip-wagon on a short run of railroad track.

'You never told us about the night shift,' Shipley growled to Satterlee.

'Didn't know about it. They must be workin' a vein while they got men still searchin' for other deposits. Long as they stay away from the powderhouse we got no worries.'

'You'll guarantee that?' snapped Cald-well.

161

In the dim light, Satterlee's face was hard as he drilled his gaze into the younger man. 'There're no guarantees in this deal, feller — only one: I guarantee you'll be dodgin' lead before it's over.'

'Quit the talk. Let's get the job done.'

Satterlee nodded curtly. 'OK, spread out. Caldwell, you stay here. Bannerman comes with me. Kid, you wait at the foot of the slope with the greaser. If Flood had come, too, we'd be sure the hosses would still be where we want 'em.'

'No time for ifs and buts now.'

They moved like shadows, the crunching of gravel under their boots deadened, even obliterated, by the noise of the mine's night shift: men yelling orders, the scrape and rattle of spoil being dumped, the rumble of the tip-wagon on the short stretch of rails.

Crouching by the heavy door set back in an alcove dug in the earth, Satterlee and Bannerman checked the padlocks. To their surprise they found all three locks open, dangling from their hasps.

'Luck's in!' whispered Satterlee.

'Or out. Could mean they're using the store, or are going to.'

That sobered Satterlee. They took the padlocks out of the hasps, set them on the ground and heaved on the door. It opened outwards and they were surprised to find three lanterns set in the wall behind thick glass, illuminating in part the store area; a safety idea used in the powder magazines of the old square-rigged battleships.

'Convenient!' Satterlee commented.

And it was. They didn't have to grope around in the dark to find what they wanted. Fuse in coils on the right, small pine boxes, interiors padded thickly with cotton, marked *Detonators*, and, stacked four high against the earthen walls, were rows of long wooden boxes stencilled with the word *Dynamite*.

They calculated that two boxes would be enough: twenty-four sticks, two boxes of detonators, and a couple of coils of fuse. They couldn't tell which was slow-burning and which was regular but Bannerman figured it wouldn't really matter: the regular fuse would be better when it came time to blast the express car safe, but the slow burner might be better here so they would be sure to be well beyond the blast when they sent this place sky high.

'It's gonna blow the mountain to dust,' Bannerman said, cutting a length of fuse over a yard long, working fast.

'So much the better,' Satterlee said, splitting two sticks of dynamite taped together and pushing a detonator into each. 'They'll never know any boxes were taken first. Gimme that fuse. Christ, cut another piece! Twice as long.'

'Can't make it too long in case someone comes in before it's reached the dynamite.'

There was no time to argue; they fitted the fuse and Bannerman touched a match to it, jumping back when it sputtered and the spark snaked swiftly down the length.

'Move!' he said. Satterlee was already ducking through the entrance. Bannerman was only a step or two behind and cannoned into the man as he stopped suddenly.

'What the hell . . . ?'

They had taken a box of dynamite each, Bannerman also had two coils of fuse over his left shoulder. Satterlee had the detonators balanced on top of his box as they went out into the night. Satterlee stopped in his tracks and Bannerman had to step around him quickly . . .

And he saw they were confronted by three men straddling the narrow way out, red light from the warning lanterns reflecting from their guns.

'You fellers ain't on this shift,' a big-shouldered man rasped. 'What you think you're doin'?'

Satterlee set down the box he was carrying on to a rock, breathing hard, wiping a hand around his sweating face. 'Foreman told us to fetch two cases. Din' say why.'

'I'm the foreman, you damn thief!'

Satterlee remained cool, shook his head, and, still panting, swept his left arm up, pointing to the main building. 'No, the other one. Day man — '

'Brinks?' the big-shouldered man said, automatically looking uphill where Satterlee pointed. 'He's got no right to — '

Satterlee's right hand swept up and his six-gun blasted swiftly. The foreman spun and cannoned into the man behind him, But the third man jumped clear and brought up his carbine. Bannerman, balancing the heavy box on his left forearm, drew and fired, having no choice.

The miner went down as Satterlee pumped two bullets into his target. Hard on the heels of the gunfire, there came the dying rumble of gravel being tipped from the wagon outside the main shaft. The sound would have covered the shooting.

Satterlee was already moving, shouldering past Bannerman who was trying to catch his box as it fell. He caught it and followed Satterlee down the hill, past the shot miners. The foreman was dead for sure. Bannerman hoped the other two were, too, because there was no time to move them.

That fuse would be burning at a fast rate inside the powder magazine — but what if some more men came down to get explosives for whatever work they were doing?

Satterlee kept moving. Bannerman cursed him, set down his box and slid the coiled fuse off his shoulder. He ran back up the slope, grabbed one of the three burning red lanterns from the entrance to the magazine and, doubled over, raced across the slope towards a tall-sided shed which stood below on flat ground near a creek. Through a hole in the roof he could see the brass smokestack of a steam-engine pulley drive, likely for driving the ore-crusher mill.

He flung the lantern as hard as he could, paused only long enough to see the flower of burning oil shower the weathered shingles, then slid and tumbled his way downslope once more. Flames rose on the roof of the engine shed.

Stumbling, he scooped up the dynamite box and fuse. He staggered away into the darkness where the others ought to be waiting now with the horses. He had to stop — for a few moments he was disoriented — then he saw the gully he was after, marked with a split shale rock that showed pale in the night.

He heard a horse coming, two horses. It was Tony Ramirez. He leaned down, took the box from Bannerman and held it across his lap as he spun his mount and spurred away.

Bannerman was still settling into leather as he urged his roan to follow.

He heard the others making their escape through the narrow defile by which they had come. As they reached the end of it there was an ear-shattering explosion. He twisted in the saddle, saw gouts of fire, rock and earth and shattered timber hurtling skywards. The blast wave struck the defile and swept through it like a hurricane, unhorsing all of the men.

Their ears were ringing and Bannerman felt himself off balance, but he caught his roan and climbed groggily into the saddle. The cases of dynamite had fallen but only one had a corner staved in. As they cleared the pass, leaving all the chaos and panic behind them, Ramirez rode up alongside.

'You set fire to their engine shed. Why, amigo? You might've died in the explosion with that delay.'

'Figured if there was a fire, most of the men would run across to put it out — get 'em off the hillside where the magazine was. Might've saved a life or two.'

Ramirez smiled thinly. 'You have not changed since the days of Juárez, amigo! They used to call you *ligero matanzaro*: the gentle killer.'

'I never heard that. Just don't see the

sense in killing innocent men if it can be avoided.'

'I think you are lucky to 'ave lived so long, eh, Heath?'

Bannermann shrugged. 'Better get after the rest although I reckon we've got plenty of time now. That explosion will keep every man there busy for a day or so.'

* * *

They reached the rendezvous about three hours late and the grey light was beginning to show the colours of the day to come when they walked their weary mounts down the precarious trail into the narrow draw.

There was only one rider back in the shadows. The creeping sunlight was reflected from an oiled rifle barrel.

Bannerman didn't recognize Mariah. He thought it was Dakota leastways or a male rider. She was dressed in a full-length poncho, with scuffed riding-boots, the male work-pants underneath flared out over the tops. She wore canvas work-gloves, a man's hat and a bandanna mask pulled up over the lower half of her face.

He guessed she was ready for the moment when they opened the express car; dressed as she was, the guards, nerves taut after being ordered to get out of the car or be blown to hell, would never recognize her as a woman. Any descriptions given to later posses would be 'six or seven masked men . . .'

She now nudged her mount into the light and put up the rifle, butt balanced on one poncho-covered thigh.

'I actually felt the ground tremble from the explosion,' she said. There was a note of relief in her voice. 'I was afraid you must've underestimated the force and were caught in it.'

'It was touch and go,' Satterlee agreed. 'Where's Dakota?'

'You're late,' she said curtly, then answered Satterlee's question. 'I sent Dakota over to that hill with the clump of brush on top. He can see the cutting from there. He'll have plenty of time to get back here before we set up the blockade.'

'Goddamit! I wanted him to have that tree cut halfway through so it'd only take another half-dozen swings of the axe to fell it across the tracks!'

Mariah tugged down the bandanna covering the lower half of her face. 'There will be plenty of time!' she said coldly. 'I-I sent him to the hill because — well, because I want to make sure the train is staying close to schedule.'

Bannerman felt himself stiffen at her words and Tony Ramirez said, '*Pardon, señorita?* But you have some . . . doubts about the train schedule? At this time?'

The others were eager for her reply and it was obvious she was uneasy, but the old Birdwood arrogance won through and she straightened, jutted her saw as she looked at them coolly. 'There is nothing lost — and perhaps something to be gained.'

'Like what?' Bannerman asked tersely. 'Finding out the train's not coming after all?'

That question brought murmurs and hard looks from the men but Mariah retained her haughty mein.

'My father always taught me to never be sure of anything — until it happened.'

'That's taking the long way round just to say you aren't even sure!'

'Damn you, Bannerman! I'm in charge! If I want to check down to the last detail, I will — without your permission or criticism.'

'Not just me you've got to worry about, Mariah.'

'No, by hell!' Satterlee's face was hard-planed and more brutal than ever in the strengthening light. 'What the hell's wrong that you haven't told us about?'

For a moment Mariah lost her haughtiness and looked uncertain. Bannerman was relentless.

'You're not as sure as you claimed about that railroad agent, are you?'

'If you hadn't killed Pat Magraw I wouldn't have had to approach John

173

Silverman! He's a family man, careful of his job. I happen to know he's having trouble paying a store bill so . . . so he agreed when I hinted he could earn himself a good deal more than what he owed the store if he let me have full details of the train's schedule. Pat would've had them, as sheriff, because, while the train was crossing this part of the county he would've had a certain responsibility to make sure it did so safely. Of course, he would have given me all the fine details. But I had to offer Silverman a bribe. He took it, but I was uneasy: he's known to have a conscience.'

'You damn well kept that to yourself,' Bannerman snapped.

'I didn't want to cause alarm but . . . just now, while there was a delay with you men coming back, I thought it wise to send Dakota to make sure the train was on schedule.'

'That sounds fair enough, Heath,' Kid Shipley said. He was a man who liked to dot all his i's and cross all his t's now he was heading into middle age.

Before anyone could answer, Jonas Flood, who had loitered on the lip of the draw called down, 'Here comes Dakota now — like Old Nick himself is after him!'

And the news was exactly what they didn't want to hear.

The train had stopped in a cutting: and there was no express car attached.

10

Raid And Run

'You damn tightwad!' Satterlee's face was full of hard, knotted muscle, jawline plainly visible, big brows drawn down and bulging, lips thin as razor edges. 'You never paid Silverman enough!'

Mariah looked down her nose at him. 'As a matter of fact I paid him a good deal more than he needed to clear his debts! And none of it comes out of your pocket!'

'You overpaid him.' All eyes turned to Bannerman as he spoke curtly. Mariah frowned. 'You gave him too much! He'd need to have a few brains to be a railroad agent, so he must've put two and two together. A heap of money to make sure he gave you the full schedule and route and stops for that special pay

176

train? Even a halfwit could figure you were planning on something happening to that train. And you confirmed it by overpaying him.'

The murmuring had a definite angry tone now and Mariah found herself backing up her horse slowly, trying to cover the look of alarm that she knew was on her face.

'You watch how you speak to Miz Birdwood, Bannerman!' Dakota was surly and even dropped a hand to his gun butt.

Bannerman ignored him, his eyes boring into the girl. 'Seems this Silverman's had a touch of conscience and wired his suspicions to his bosses. To play it safe they changed the schedule. There'd be a lot of money on that train: army backpay. They couldn't afford to take any chances. Now our plans are as stale as yesterday's bunkhouse beans.'

'Where is the damn express van, anyway?' Satterlee growled. 'That's what I want to know. Silverman couldn't've gotten any word to them before the train was already travellin' — with the express van hooked on. So where the hell is it? They must've shunted it off somewheres.'

They were looking at Jonas Flood now. Frowning, he drew his maps and plans out of his saddle-bags, did some shuffling, then studied one section of a map that covered the country where they were now. He suddenly stabbed at the paper, almost driving his finger through it.

'Here! Before it reached that cuttin' where Dakota says it's stopped now, there's a switch point and a siding that connects with an old spur track.' He peered closer, moving so his shadow didn't fall across the map. 'Yeah. Looks like it could be still passable, and it seems to hook up with the main line at a place called Septimo . . . ?'

He glanced at Mariah and she shook her head. 'Ghost town. Long abandoned. There was a minor gold strike but it petered out. Railroad ran tracks in but lost a lot of money when it failed to produce. As far as I know the tracks are still there; they could still be usable. I suppose, with a little luck, they might even get a train on to the main line ahead of the one we've been waitin' for by going the long way round through the old Septimo loop.'

'How the hell they gonna move that express car?' Caldwell wanted to know. 'Push it?'

'If Silverman's conscience bucked him early enough they could have got another train on its way from Pine Bluffs. There're railroad workshops there.'

They all stared at Flood's announcement.

'And you just recollected that!' Satterlee said threateningly. 'Never took it into consideration that what's just happened could actually happen and foul us up!'

'Cool down,' Bannerman said. 'There was no reason to expect this snag when Flood drew up his plans. We believed we had all the right info to ourselves.'

Mariah flushed under his accusing gaze. She shook herself. 'All right! It's happened! Now, *what do we do*?'

'Whatever it is, *señorita*, it should be very soon!' Tony Ramirez pointed to the still rising sun. 'If they tapped into the telegraph line last night there could be another train on its way now to pick up the express van. It may even have been travelling most of the night towards that siding.'

'Then what the hell we standin' around here for?' snapped Kid Shipley. 'Jesus! What a mess!' He raked his eyes round the group and let his gaze come to rest on Mariah and Dakota. 'Swore I'd never work with amateurs again after I lost my brother followin' someone else's plan, and here I'm doin' the same thing again! Except I don't have no big brother to lose now.'

'But we all have big money to stuff our pockets!' Flood's clipped tones brought their attention to him. 'The train in the cutting will be used as a decoy now. They'll send it on, and while we're wastin' time tryin' to run it down, the rescue train — more than likely already well on its way — will hitch up the express van on the siding and take it along the old abandoned line through Septimo.'

'And you can bet both trains will be crammed with soldiers or posse men,' Bannerman pointed out. 'It's going to be a helluva lot harder than our original plan, now they're alerted.'

Josh Caldwell was looking at the giant tree they aimed to cut down and drop across the tracks. 'This tree's got a twin brother.' He pointed along the rim of the draw to a similar large tree but with more foliage. 'How about instead of wastin' time usin' an axe, we shove a couple sticks of dynamite down among the roots and drop *both* across the rails.'

'What's the point?' growled Satterlee. 'One's all that's needed. They're nigh on two hundred yards apart — '

'A little longer than our train with its

181

wagons and cars — minus the express van,' Caldwell said with a crooked grin. 'We drop one in front, the other behind — the train's trapped. And so are any soldiers on board!'

'Mebbe they got a car full of horses,' Kid Shipley suggested.

'Mebbe,' conceded Caldwell, face alight with excitement now. 'But even if we only delay a dozen soldiers it's that many fewer for us to worry about.'

'Why? What the hell we s'posed to be doin'?'

'Use your head, Wiley. We go after the express van on the switch siding.'

'And we'd better do that right now,' Bannerman pointed out. 'Two men stay here to set the charges for the trees, the rest of us get to that van — before reinforcements arrive from Pine Bluffs.'

The prospect of action, and putting the modified plan into operation, animated the group and it was quickly decided that Caldwell could handle the blasting down of the big trees by himself while the rest tackled the still isolated express van.

'With some luck, we'll have broken it open before the new lot of soldiers arrive,' Mariah said, eyes bright now.

'And mebbe we'll find out at last just what's in that special vault — besides all the money you promised will be there.'

Suddenly her eyes were cold. She gave him the bleak stare for a long moment, then said.

'Well, you won't find out anything standing around here!'

She wheeled her mount away, the big poncho billowing about her slim body; then the others were racing for their own horses.

* * *

Caldwell planted three sticks of dynamite under each tree — two behind to destroy the massive root system, and one in front below the rim so the ground would be blown outwards and topple the tree towards the tracks below.

Detonators were in place, lengths of fuse connected; he would wait until he could see the train's approach before cutting the fuses, judging their length and burning rate against the estimated speed of the approaching train. He had had lots of experience at doing this kind of thing and was confident he could drop those giant trees exactly where he wanted them — and at the right time.

He could see a thickening column of smoke rising out of the cutting where Dakota said the train was stopped. It was getting up steam. He felt the usual tension knotting his belly as the minutes dragged by and there was still no sign of the train leaving the cutting. He couldn't cut the fuses to length until the train was properly under way and settled into a constant speed.

His hands were shaking; it had been a while between jobs. He smiled crookedly. The last time had been intended to be exactly that: *the last time*. He had met and married Carrie just before the job was due but had already given his word that he would act as the explosives man on a raid on the biggest Wells Fargo Express office at that time, in Deadwood.

Why not do the job? Get a nest egg, then 'retire' and set up a 'normal' marriage, raise kids like Carrie wanted, get a few acres of river-bottom land . . .

The idea had sounded good and he had lied to her for the first time, claiming he had committed to a job at a mine, which he couldn't renege on. She had been understanding, not very keen on losing her new husband for a few weeks, but had given her approval.

Then the whole damn thing had gone about as wrong as it could. The express office caught fire and burned down the night before the job was to be pulled. So it was immediately abandoned — and that was that.

He found out how hard it was to scratch together a few dollars to support a wife — already pregnant — and was getting pretty desperate when Flood had contacted him about this deal. It seemed the answer to his prayers, though he wasn't much of a praying man.

Now there had been complications but at least there was still a chance he could come out with more than enough *dinero* for Carrie and the kid, when it came, and he would settle into a stress-free family life . . .

'God almighty!'

He jumped to his feet amongst the rocks where he had been sitting, waiting for the train to appear so he could judge the speed. It came swaying out of the cutting, whistle shrieking, and he counted the rocking cars automatically, he realized there *was* an express car this side of the caboose!

'How the hell . . . ?'

He was so surprised, after Dakota saying so certainly that the van had been shunted on to a switch-point siding, that he almost forgot the fuses. Then he shook himself, made a reasonable estimate of the speed, did a quick calculation with the known burning rate and hacked with his jack-knife. He cut a shorter length for the tree that would topple across the track ahead of the train, to allow for the delay as brakes were applied and the whole train coming together with a series of violent clanks, sliding on the rails. He would adjust for the second tree, which he thought was going to be a little too far back, more than he would have liked, but as long as it hemmed in the train . . .

He ducked as the fuses sputtered, and as he did so he stared at that 'express van'. He suddenly smiled.

It wasn't the express van! He could see it now: a box car painted in the Wells Fargo colours — roughly, too! They must've done it last night with paint from one of the cargo wagons: red, yellow and black, even a couple of white curlicues in the corners. It gleamed and shone brightly like new metal in the sun. It was freshly done, all right! While the train was in the cutting.

The real van was still on that

switch-point siding. This was meant as a crude decoy so the raiders would chase the train while the relief train hitched up to the real express van and cut down the abandoned line to Septimo . . .

'Almost fooled us, you sonuvers!' Caldwell said aloud. He ducked as the dynamite under the first tree exploded amongst the roots, immediately followed by the crack of the single stick below the rim. The giant tree toppled immediately, dirt and rocks erupting as the shattered roots tore away.

He rose up, saw the streams of sparks spurting from under the locomotive's wheels as the engineer applied his brakes in a panic. Then the tree bounced and thudded, ripped out a length of railroad track, twisted a second length and settled in a cloud of dust. He heard as well as saw the train shudder its full length as it rammed into the immovable barrier.

A few moments later the yells of the men on board the train, who no doubt were being flung violently around, were drowned by the thundering crash of the second tree. One branch smashed the rear end of the caboose, splinters hurtling and thrumming through the air.

Then there was only smoke and steam and derailed cars: not overturned, but with the wheels jumping off track. The entire train was trapped between the massive trees, out of commission.

It was time to join the others.

*　*　*

They might have known the guards with the real express car would not be sitting around playing poker for matches or cigarettes.

These were hand-picked men, with top army records for fighting, vigilance and devotion to duty. They were intensely aware that they were charged with guarding backpay for their comrades-in-arms — and also for themselves. Each knew the grinding privation caused by hit-or-miss army paydays . . .

Alerted that there would be an attempt to rob the express van, the twelve armed guards riding with it immediately formed three groups of four, each taking shifts of four hours on, four off. It was hot in the sealed van and they had the roof ventilator's blades open all the way, as were the loopholes.

If a man needed to relieve himself, it was agreed that during the long, dark hours the doors would remain locked; someone said — boasting a little — that if a man was well-enough endowed he could use one of the loopholes and there was much jibing and ribaldry as every man claimed he could manage such an awkward position 'without any trouble'. The four men who returned with wet trousers were given such a ribbing that the off-duty men trying to sleep complained to the point where blows came mighty close to being thrown.

It was the tough Irish sergeant, Liam O'Kelly, who saw the first of the raiders working their way into the draw where the switch-point rails backed up to the rock wall. It had seemed a good move to manhandle the heavy van as close as possible to this wall, leaving one side that they wouldn't have to worry about guarding or defending. But when they heard the soft thuds of boots on the armoured roof, they knew that all they had done was to offer easy access to the van's roof for the raiders.

'Ah, sweet Jasus! Here they come — and they're atop of us already!'

One man, wakened with a fright by the sergeant's bellow, in his half-alert state snatched his rifle and fired into the curve of the roof. The men dropped and hugged the floor, dived into every nook and cranny they could, as the bullet ricocheted from the inner armour plating.

O'Kelly didn't hesitate; his own rifle butt came up and dropped the startled guard as he began to climb out of his bedroll. 'Hell an' limbo, you daft bastard, Doherty, so ye are! What'd you do that for?'

Doherty was nursing his swelling, throbbing head. He shook it silently, unable to reply. He earned plenty of abuse from the men already at loopholes.

'I see three!' a very dark-skinned man yelled, and his rifle blasted through a loophole.

There was answering fire and they heard with satisfaction the thud of bullets hitting the reinforced sides.

But O'Kelly's attention was on the roof.

He could hear nails or bolts tearing loose up there.

They were wasting their time trying to rip the roof off because of the inner armour plating which was separated from the regular roof by a couple of inches. But . . .

There was a clatter and he recognized it as the cap of one of the ventilators. At the same time a shaft of strong sunlight beamed down into the van where the armour plate had been cut through to allow for the ventilator — *their only weakness!* And these vile sons of bitches had found it!

O'Kelly lunged forward, knocking aside two guards who stood directly in the beam of sunlight, and fired three fast shots up the ventilator shaft. He heard a very satisfying grunt and the clatter of a body falling. He grinned, showing his worn-down teeth, rotten from army food and bad dental hygiene.

'That's what's waitin' for every man who tries to come in! Show some sense, lads. Ye can't bust yer way in here!'

'Maybe not, Paddy,' answered Bannerman, shouting to be heard over the gunfire from both inside and outside the van. Kid Shipley was lying on the curved tarpaper-covered roof of the van with Ramirez kneeling beside him, trying to stanch the flow of blood from two bullet wounds — one under his right collar-bone, the other in his neck.

'But we've got something for you!'

Bannerman yelled this last and O'Kelly stepped into the light, his rifle coming up. But the big Irish sergeant paused with the lever only halfway cycled.

'Holy Mother! Get down, lads, down for Chris'sakes!'

He was lying flat, rolling away from underneath the ventilator as the bundle of dynamite with the sputtering fuse came swinging into view on the end of a string. There was a mad scramble as the other guards tried to get out of the way.

'Open the door!'

'Open the goddamn door!'

'Sarge!'

'Holy Mary, Mother of God . . . ' one man started praying.

'Jesus Christ, Sarge! *Unlock the freakin' door or we're all dead*!'

Liam O'Kelly was well aware of that and fumbled for the key. But knew he would be too late: by the time he had unlocked the two heavy padlocks, slid the door back enough to let the men through, the fuse would have reached

194

the dynamite and the blast wave would . . .

Well, it didn't bear thinking about what it would do, distributing their body parts, all round the armoured van, dripping from the walls. *Ugh!* Brady had the right idea, the only worthwhile one: praying was all a man could do now.

Then he froze and watched, fascinated, as the dynamite with its fuse burning within a few inches of the detonator was whisked back up the shaft. And the same deep voice called down.

'That was just a teaser, boys: what *could* happen unless you unlock the sliding door and stand in the opening with your hands in the air. You'll be covered, of course, by our men waiting outside. Do I hear keys turning in the locks?'

'All right, you bleddy bastard! Ye give us no choice!'

'That's the idea, Paddy. Now, I've got a vesta held against the last few inches of fuse. Better have the door open in one minute or you can share this dynamite among you.'

In less than a minute the big door slid back and the guards stood there, empty hands raised shoulder high. They were covered by the rifles and shotguns held by Dakota and Mariah and Wiley Satterlee.

'Here's Josh,' Dakota said, using his head to point at Caldwell riding in.

'Get those guards tied up!' Bannerman called down from the roof. He looked at Mariah, disguised in her poncho and with her bandanna masking her lower face, his own face and those of the others were similarly masked. 'Man hurt bad. Can't stop the bleeding.'

She nudged Dakota, not wanting to speak, although she had been practising using a deeper, more mannish voice. The hardcase said, 'Lower him down — we'll see what we can do.'

The guards were ordered to jump down and they silently submitted to being bound. Before the gag was tied over his mouth, O'Kelly looked into Mariah's eyes, frowned a little, and said,

'Ye're in bad comp'ny, me darlin'. I was you, I'd quit very quickly. Ye'll never get that safe open.'

She rammed the knotted rag brutally into his mouth and he made guttural sounds as she tightened it as hard as she could. She did not take kindly to having been recognized as a woman, despite her attempt at disguise.

Caldwell placed the dynamite in position around the huge safe door, having his doubts that it would be effective. As the fuse burned and they hunkered down behind some boulders, he said to Bannerman,

'I've read about the new Hemersley-Bayliss vaults. There are rods inside on springs. The blast dislodges wedges and the springs drive the rods forward into cavities cut into the safe's body. Locks the door solid, as if it was welded in place . . . '

Bannerman looked at him quickly.

'This is one of those?'

'Not sure, but I think so. It's only got 'H/B' on the door medallion, but . . . Duck!'

The explosion was loud and vast amounts of paper and splintered stools, abandoned rifles and spare uniforms and coats were flung — the uniforms and coats already smouldering — through the open van doors. The van rocked and one corner of the roof lifted. Some outside planks bulged and splintered but did not loosen from their fastenings. The roar was deafening and smoke billowed.

The interior of the van was on fire when the raiders could see and hear again. One of the bound and gagged guards had a shattered length of wood driven through his thigh and he writhed and made choking sounds of pain through his gag. They could hear the horses, tethered out of sight, whinnying and no doubt trying to tear away their hitching ropes.

'How the hell we gonna get that fire

out?' Satterlee demanded, holding a bent arm across his eyes to protect them from the strengthening heat blast.

Caldwell looked at him soberly. 'Won't matter. Look at the safe.'

The huge metal safe still stood upright, though two long bolts that had held it tightly against one wall were loosened. The big door was still closed, one hinge bent.

Otherwise the massive unit was un-touched. The lock seemed as solid as ever.

'*Señors*,' said Tony Ramirez as he climbed on to a rock. 'I think it is time to leave!'

He pointed at a band of horsemen coming out of the cutting where the train had been imprisoned by the blasted-down trees.

There were at least ten riders, obviously back-up guards who had been riding the train with a van full of saddled horses, waiting in case someone was foolish enough to attempt a raid.

And the raid had been attempted. And it had failed.

Now it was time to run.

11

Scattered

The shooting started before they had reached the getaway mounts.

And not just from guns from the charging posse.

Bannerman was helping Ramirez hastily bind Kid Shipley's wounds when he heard a single shot close by. Crouching, he whirled, swinging his rifle up, ready instinctively.

Dakota was standing over the big Irish sergeant with a smoking gun: O'Kelly had a bullet hole smashed into the side of his head.

Bannerman's eyes narrowed, but widened when he saw Mariah handing Dakota the reins of his getaway mount.

The surly hardcase mounted, wheeled away with the woman and spurred across the slope.

Bannerman lifted his rifle to his shoulder but hesitated with his finger curling around the trigger. *Settle it later — now was the time to move . . .*

Kid Shipley moaned and groaned and thrashed so hard they couldn't hold him and he half-tumbled as they tried to set him down. He ripped out a ragged oath, gasping, as he looked up at them.

'Leave. I'll never — stay on — a — hoss. Go! Chris'sakes — go!'

Ramirez glanced at Bannerman who, after a moment's hesitation, knowing Shipley spoke the truth, reached down and squeezed the wounded man's good shoulder.

'Been a long trail, Kid.'

'End now. Git! Lemme have my — gun . . .'

Ramirez slid Shipley's Colt from the man's holster, placed it in his good hand, cocked. '*Adios*, amigo.'

Shipley, his face contorted in pain, made an impatient gesture with his head, wincing. As the Mexican and

Bannerman ran for their mounts, rifle bullets whistled overhead, thudded into the ground, one wild shot ricocheting from the side of the half-wrecked express van.

Shipley began shooting at the spread-out posse men as his companions rode away, not wasting time or ammunition shooting back . . .

When they swung out of the siding, Bannerman turned his head slightly and got a peripheral view of Kid Shipley holding his Colt in both hands, tracking one rider. The gun bucked and almost jumped from his grip. The rider seemed untouched but the man beside him cut loose with a shotgun and Shipley's body was slammed along the ground, limbs flopping loosely.

Bannerman turned to the front again and lashed the roan with the rein ends, although the mount was giving its best already.

He had an impression of the others scattering across the countryside, glimpsed the billowing poncho disappearing over a rise with Dakota hard behind. His knee pressure turned the roan slightly in that direction but he was forced to swing back on to his original track when two riders slanted towards him.

Their guns smoked, just puffs of grey-blue ripped away by the wind of their passage. He heard the air-whip of one bullet, had no idea where the second had gone. But he was a target now.

These two had selected him out of the scattering robbers and were joined by a third rider as Bannerman jumped the roan over a deadfall. He rocked in the saddle, was almost unseated as the roan's forefeet skidded on thick grass. It righted itself and raced on, experienced at flight, but ground had been lost.

Ramirez had disappeared. So had Mariah and Dakota. He didn't expect to see Wiley Satterlee; the man was more than adept at saving his own skin and had been the first mounted and away the moment the posse had been sighted. Josh Caldwell was a dark speck on a bare slope, three or four men after him, but, even as Bannerman watched two veered away and there was Jonas Flood, a good planner and fine shot, but a lousy rider, fighting his mount down into a broken-sided draw.

There was a cloud of dust and Flood's arm lifted wildly as man and horse spilled over the edge.

The two posse men lashed wildly at their mounts as they closed in swiftly.

Bannerman started to turn in that direction but a bullet fanned his face so closely that he was almost unhorsed. Clutching wildly at the horn, throwing his weight against the direction of the fall, he just managed to stay in leather. Then he was in a boulderfield, lead ricocheting savagely, lifting dust from a big granite egg beside him.

These men must have been hand-picked for the back-up guard chore on that pay-train. And they were shooting to kill.

He had a knotted feeling deep in his belly, at the same time as the disturbing thought penetrated his brain: they might be lucky to escape with their lives!

He weaved the roan between rocks, trying not to make a pattern out of it. See a gap, lunge for it. Next time lunge past a similar gap, maybe swerve abruptly around a large rock and race off in a direction at a very sharp angle. Twice it worked and the pursuers thundered on.

He gained more than a hundred yards the second time, and slipped over a rise while the men were still weaving and cursing, looking for him in the boulderfield.

It looked like a fairly clear run from here, but there was a deep fold in the hills that he wasn't going to be able to avoid; a perfect place for ambush . . .

He eased the Colt in his holster, managed to fumble some shells from his belt loops and, dropping two — *Goddamnittohell!* — slid three through the rifle's loading gate.

A yell from behind.

The sons of bitches had him spotted!

The sweating, grunting roan reacted to the hard touch of the spurs with a snort and a game leap forward, down into the treacherous shadows of the fold between the hills.

★　★　★

Jonas Flood knew, with heart thudding as if it would smash through his ribs, that this was it: trail's end.

His brain was spinning, wild thoughts swirling, but shattering pain was confusing him, too, where he had hit his head in his fall from his mount.

The animal was struggling vainly in its efforts to rise: one foreleg had snapped. The posse men would arrive very soon. *Hell! Here they were!*

The riders came thundering over the edge of the draw, ten yards to the left, hitting a slope of loose earth left by some past washaway. Obviously they knew the area better than Flood but, reeling a little, he picked up his rifle out of the dirt, shook it free of dust and sighted quickly. He fired, lever working twice.

The lead rider's horse whinnied and shied sideways, bullet-burned. The rider was caught off balance and had to leap from the saddle. His companion hauled rein and tried to lift his own rifle, one-handed, but the horse was still sliding and he too toppled out of the saddle.

Then Flood's suffering mount reared on its hind quarters and, toppling, fell against him. He was knocked flying, lost the rifle, rolled down the slope to the bottom. Half-blinded by grit, his head spinning worse than ever, the rifle almost buried under sliding waves of loose soil, Jonas Flood's legs worked under him and carried him in a desperate zigzag away from the downed posse men.

One man was on his knees, triggering his Colt, the bullets whining, gouging stones and dust from the side of the narrow draw. Flood was not a man of action, tough enough, sure, but he was not fit like Bannerman and Satterlee and most of the gunfighters.

The long-serving, battle-hardened soldier posse men had muscles and tendons like iron; also they were years younger.

Flood knew his luck had run out but he didn't aim to just give up. He could throw down his gun, lift his hands and it was possible they wouldn't kill him on the spot. Possible, but by no means certain.

Or he could give as good an account of himself as he was able. He was The Planner: and now was the time for a plan that would save his neck.

Unfortunately, he didn't have one.

He took another tumble, skidding on loose gravel as he staggered around a rock. Instead of fighting the fall he went with it this time, kept rolling, came up on his shoulders and then twisted on to his knees, gun blazing.

Where the hell were they . . . ?

The question screamed through his

throbbing head as he saw his wasted bullets kicking dust from the broken walls. There was no sign of the soldiers.

Then a voice spoke from just above him: 'You just run outta luck, you murderin' bastard!'

Flood reacted instinctively, throwing himself left and downwards, as a gun thundered from the rim. He felt the bite of lead in his back, under the right shoulder blade. He transferred his gun to his other hand, fumbling. That was when the second man appeared in front of him, dusty, sweat-glistening, boots spread firmly, and his gun coming up for the kill.

The soldiers emptied their guns into Flood.

* * *

Mariah discarded the full-length poncho.

It was too hot, too heavy, and slowed down her escape, its bulk acting like a sail all aback on a ship as she flogged her weary mount on.

Dakota was not only keeping up to protect her, but while she rested briefly, he rode to the highest observation point and watched the backtrail.

'Seems to be more of 'em,' he reported back one time.

'Probably joined by the ones we had tied up.'

Dakota frowned, sceptical. 'Or maybe that second train's arrived and they brought half the the damn army with 'em.'

She gulped water from her nearly empty canteen, wiped her wet jaw. 'We've got to get back to Crown! Someone besides that Irishman might've seen I was a woman. I need to be back at the ranch and have my alibi ready in case — '

'Me, too.' Dakota said it flatly, looking steadily at her.

'Of course,' she agreed. But there had been that slight hesitation and he knew that, as usual, she was thinking of nobody but herself.

He was loyal to her, because Old Darby had made him swear he would protect her and all that was Crown for as long as he lived. He had admired Darby, maybe even envied him, and he would stick by his word.

But, just once in a while it would be nice if she showed him some small amount of appreciation . . .

'Well?' she snapped suddenly, making him start. 'Have you got any kind of a plan?'

'Wish I did. What the hell kind a plan can you have with the whole damn country crawlin' with soldiers who want nothin' better'n than to kill us?'

'Damn you, Dakota! You get me back to Crown! Quickly!'

'We'll get there,' he said with tired confidence. 'But you gonna be a lot thirstier and hungrier before we do. So, best put the stopper back in that canteen.'

She had been lifting it towards her mouth for another drink. She checked at his warning. Then, deliberately, she took a long pull.

'There's plenty of water between here and Crown!'

'Sure. You think they won't be waitin' at every muddy hoofprint an' rockpool? Don't even think about the river or the creeks. They'll have camps along them.'

She stamped her foot, frustrated, angry that the hold-up had failed — and so she was staring ruin in the face.

'Just do your job!'

'Will, if you let me. We can't stay here. With the men they've got out there they'll close off this area in ten minutes.'

'Then what're we waiting for?'

He sighed and turned towards his foam-streaked mount as she hurried to her own horse.

Crown seemed a long, long way off.

* * *

Bannerman and Tony Ramirez tried to stick together — leastways, within sight of each other — but it was too dangerous.

The posse had obviously been

212

reinforced by riders on fresh mounts and there were enough men combing the country now to make it risky to go in pairs.

Reining down on top of a broken ridge, Tony, in the shadow of a long, leaning rock, gestured to the plains below where there seemed to be moving dots wherever they looked.

'They form a long line and make a sweep in this direction — and I think, amigo, we are in even more trouble.'

Bannerman nodded. 'Second train must've been crammed with soldiers. Parting of the ways, Tony.'

There was no time for sentiment, even if they had been the kind of men who would indulge in such a thing. They shook hands briefly.

'See you in Durango, sometime.'

'You recall the *Rojo Escorpio*?'

'The Red Scorpion? Not likely to forget it — we nearly bought the farm. Lucky, that girl having a *teniente* boyfriend in the town patrol and letting us slip out.'

'One of my . . . cousins now owns it. She can be trusted. We meet there sometime, eh? *Mañana*?'

'It'll be a long time till 'tomorrow', amigo. But I'll try.' Bannerman touched a hand to his hatbrim. '*Hasta luego.*'

'*Vaya con Dios, compadre.*'

They cleared the crest in moments, going their separate ways, each knowing the other would, as a matter of course, lay false trails, misleading the pursuit, giving each other the best possible chance. The way of *compadres*.

12

Ready and Waiting

Josh Caldwell had found a way out.

He wasn't a praying man but he thanked God for guiding him through the wild country where pursuit had driven him, and into the safety of the horizon-stretching Laramie Plains.

He could be forewarned here, see any posse coming for miles. What was best was that the Medicine Bows were a long way behind him now and he was south of McFadden and Rock Springs, north of Laramie, with the Albany cut-off ahead and the Chugwater Crossing of the Laramie River within easy reach.

Make that crossing and there was the sanctuary of the Laramie Mountains within a few miles.

He still didn't know how he had

found his way here; there had been so much twisting and turning through canyons and sunken draws, low hills, a big spread of brushwood that had given him shelter as the pursuers beat it flat in their wild search for him, eventually setting it afire.

They did him an unintentional favour there; the wall of flames reared so high that it beat back the hunters, while the rolling wall of thick smoke gave Caldwell all the cover he needed to make the long run away from the area. He chuckled to himself as he slaked his thirst alongside his trail-weary mount, upstream from the crossing.

At last, his heart was slowing down; it had been beating wildly and erratically since things had gone wrong at the express van. No money was a bitter pill to swallow, but: Money or your life?

Somehow he had been given the choice, and now he was reconciled to returning home with empty pockets. But the main thing was that he *was* returning home. To Carrie and the child, which should have been born by now . . . a son! he hoped.

He sluiced water over his head and face, let it trickle inside his sweat-damp shirt, feeling some of the accumulated grit wash away. It would be nice if he could get back to Crown and pick up that $500 cash Mariah had given each of them upon arrival; he had hidden the money under a loose board beside one of his bunk's rear legs . . .

No! He wouldn't push his luck. He had a chance of surviving this ordeal now and he wouldn't throw it away. His family was more important than a fistful of dollars. Sure, it would be a harder grind, but somehow they would make it, the three of them — himself, Carrie and the kid: *Jared*. He had decided to name him after his father, Jared Caldwell. Had a good ring to it. Would look good on a shingle of some sort, say a . . . a doctor's? An attorney's? He chuckled at this. Fancy him siring a future attorney at law! And him a man who hadn't respected the law for more than half his life . . .

One day, he would tell Carrie about this moment, and she would laugh — that fine, tinkling feel-good sound she made, all warm and pink, eyes bright with happiness. It was real pain to know it would be at least a week before he heard that welcoming laugh of hers.

He died with that thought. Never heard the crack of the Creedmoor sniper's rifle fired by the prone soldier behind one of the smallest bushes on the flat plain across the river. The bullet took the side of Caldwell's head off and as he spilled into the river, his horse snorting and leaping away, the soldier rolled on to his side and waved his hat, calling,

'You was right, Lieutenant. He did use the smoke as cover to get out here. Can pack up now an' go home. 'Less you want to bury him . . . ?'

'Leave the son of a bitch to rot!' the officer called back from his hiding-place. 'Let's go find the other bastards.'

They almost got Bannerman.

Five soldiers, grimy and hard-faced, had likely been told about the cold-blooded murder of Sergeant O'Kelly, with all the gory details, and a few added for good measure.

They were all shooting to kill.

They were good, he had to give them that. He had approached the waterhole quietly, afoot, leading the thirsty roan, having to quiet it down a few times with a swift hand over the quivering muzzle as it scented water. The canteen had been empty a long time.

After ground-hitching the roan, which had at last remembered its training and was now doing its best to hold back its instinctive urge to run towards the waiting water, Bannerman checked his rifle and six-gun before bellying up to the bush that he would use as shelter while he studied the waterhole.

It wasn't large, about six feet in diameter, shaded at one end by a stand of rocks with a couple of straggly trees leaning outwards. That would be the side any traveller would make for, where the water was coolest. So he checked it out carefully, moving only his eyes, pausing at every twitch of a blade of grass, the slight bending of a spindly weed-stalk under the weight of a line of hard-working ants, the passing breeze, or the swirl of wind from a swooping hawk as its talons sought the ground for mice and lizards.

The sun was hot on his back. Sweat trickled down his face and neck, stung his eyes. Maybe it was when he wiped his eyes quickly with the back of a wrist that he missed something. He had no warning that anyone was there, apart from himself and the roan, as he rose warily, rifle in both hands, crouching, tense and ready to spring away from danger.

Next thing he knew he was lying on his back, hat hanging by its tie-thong caught under his chin. His head was ringing and he felt hot liquid around his left ear. Even before searching finger-tips told him he had lost most of the lobe on that ear, long-honed self-preservation instincts rolled him swiftly back behind the bush. It shook with a volley of shots and grit kicked into his face.

His body convulsed as he flung himself back and down, glimpsing the men with bushes and grass tied to their heads and bodies, rising out of the shadows at the far end of the waterhole.

He stopped rolling and flung himself towards them, bellydown. *They weren't expecting that!*

His rifle cracked in three fast shots, moving slightly after each one, the lever working smoothly. His lead found three targets; maybe none was fatal, but three men yelled in varying degrees of sudden pain. One rolled into the water, thrashing. A man in the rocks leapt up, startled, but recovered, came spinning towards Bannerman, firing two wild shots.

Bannerman triggered even as he

rolled back, he saw the man's rifle jump from his hands. Then he threw himself at the roan which was readying to run. He grabbed the horn, felt the strong, hard-working body swing away, the hard edge of the saddle biting into the arch of his ribs. His boots thudded alongside for a few wild seconds. With a heavy grunt he kicked up and swung his legs at the same time, getting one over the heaving back.

The roan was ten yards past his end of the waterhole before he managed to settle into the saddle and stay low, fumbling for the reins. Rifle fire rattled raggedly behind him, eruptions of gravel and dead leaves rose up ahead and to one side, marking where the shots went.

He wheeled away towards the timbers; they had anticipated this move if the ambush failed and he had got back to his horse.

Two men came to the edge of the trees. One dropped to one knee, sighting carefully. The other, mounted, spurred in, revolver hammering. Bannerman weaved, triggered the rifle and hit the man on the ground, the bullet knocking him sprawling. He crawled back into the shelter of the trees in obvious pain.

By that time the other man had emptied his pistol and was veering away. Bannerman went after him, rifle held out to one side for balance as the roan raced in. The soldier hadn't expected the move and, flustered, wild-eyed, hipped in his saddle and hurled the empty gun at Bannerman.

The gunfighter dodged and the gun fell harmlessly to the ground. The roan was starting to veer off. He yanked it back in line as the soldier stood in his stirrups, rifle half-drawn from its scabbard, fear streaking his white face. The big roan crashed into the slimmer black filly and knocked it off its feet.

There were wild whinnies and Bannerman was hard put to stay in saddle, but he managed it and swung his rifle. The barrel cracked across the side of the soldier's head and knocked him sprawling even as the filly went down, thrashing. Bannerman wheeled the roan away and the wounded man on the ground tried to get up, fumbling at his pistol. Bannerman's boot caught him under the jaw and lifted him five feet before he crashed to the ground.

By then Bannerman was hauling rein. He leapt off and ran to the shaken filly as it stood up, quivering. In a deft movement he lifted the big army saddle canteen over the horn, glad to see that it hadn't been crushed in the fall. Then he caught the panting roan's reins and clambered back into leather.

The men he had wounded back at the waterhole were shooting desultorily as he rode off, well out of range.

He had no trouble shaking them off. He stopped a couple of miles away to take a good long drink from the canteen and to give the roan a hatful.

That was when he heard distant gunfire, and, as it faded, also a woman's scream.

Dakota was dead, shot in the back of the head.

His gun was on the ground within a foot of his lifeless fingers. He lay on his back, staring sightlessly up at the sky, the ground beneath him darkening with the spread of his blood.

Mariah Birdwood stood rigidly beside him, staring down fixedly, the back of her hand to her mouth, bleeding where her teeth had bitten into the flesh. She wrenched her gaze away from the dead man and turned quickly as gravel crunched under boots.

Wiley Satterlee sauntered up, a smoking revolver in his right hand down at his side. He had lost the plaster covering the gash on his face when he had dragged down his bandanna mask after the safe had failed to open in the express car.

The line that ran from under his left eye to his jawline was red and angry-looking, the seven stitches evenly spaced. Part of the wound had opened and was oozing some sort of discharge. She looked away hurriedly.

Satterlee noticed and put up his left hand to touch the wound, wincing involuntarily.

'Yeah, that goddam Bannerman! Marked me for life! Every lousy dodger they put out on me now will either show this scar or describe it! Son of a bitch!'

She was trembling, still wiping at grey and red ooze that had splashed on her when Satterlee's murderous bullet had smashed into Dakota's skull. She felt sick to her stomach despite all the years of an active ranch life where blood and gore, mostly on animals, was a daily feature. But to see someone who had been close for so many years, mutilated and . . .

'You gonna throw up?' Satterlee's harsh, yet casual question gave her strength she didn't know she had. She rounded on him suddenly, not realizing what she was doing, clawing at his face.

A fingernail caught a stitch in the wound and tore it out. Blood flowed.

Wiley Satterlee let out a roaring yell of agony and lashed out, his left fist catching her on the side of the jaw. She dropped to her knees, tilted sideways, close to losing consciousness. In her agony she saw him draw back a boot. As he was about to deliver the blow Bannerman came out of the rocks, rifle in hand, bloody bandanna covering his ear.

'Don't do that, Wiley!'

Satterlee stopped the movement so abruptly he actually teetered on his toes. His face changed, eyes widened, seeming to blaze at Bannerman.

'Well. Now this is just about perfect! If only we'd blowed that safe and had us a snootful of *dinero!* But I'll settle for this.' Suddenly he grinned crookedly. 'Was wonderin' where I could find you and square our leetle difficulty, Bannerman. An' here you are.'

'Dakota doesn't look anything like me.'

'Huh? Aw, no, I never mistook him for you. I meant to kill that son of a bitch. Never took to him. Did you?'

He sounded as if he really wanted to know.

'Didn't bother me much.'

'He ain't gonna bother no one now. I never liked the sonuver. I needed the gal, anyways.'

Bannerman was genuinely surprised. 'Mariah? Why?'

Satterlee grinned crookedly. 'Well, knowin' you an' your queer ways an' codes, I figured if I had her with me, you'd come after me — to rescue her. Recollect I told you once, you oughta ride a white hoss like that feller in the suit of armour in that ol'-fashioned story . . .'

'You aimed to use her to get me to come after you — so we could settle our differences?' Bannerman shook his head slowly. 'I never cared all that much for Mariah.' The dazed girl looked up and frowned, her face hardening as the words sunk in.

But she couldn't quite disguise the cloud of fear there, too.

Satterlee reached down suddenly and hauled her to her feet, pulling her in front of him, clamping her as a protective shield with his left arm.

His Colt was in his right hand.

'Now, reckon you won't shoot through her just to get to me!'

'Just told you, I never thought much of Mariah. Too arrogant, too bossy, not my type.'

The girl's swollen lips curled. 'Do you think I'd ever have anything to do with you? A common gunslinger I could buy for a few dollars?'

'However many dollars are offered, they won't buy *me*. My gun, for a time, sure, but not me. I told you that.'

Satterlee laughed. 'See? Told you he had queer notions. You ain't all that popular, sis, but he still won't shoot through you to get at me, which gives me a whole lot of advantage. Said I'd git you any way I could, Heath.'

Bannerman nodded towards the

unsheathed Colt. 'You want me to draw against a naked gun. Already cocked, I see.'

'Sounds good to me. Way I'll tell it, it was a square-off, leathered guns, an' I beat you flat, keep up my reputation. Bit sneaky but, hell! What you say to that?'

'How about *shoot*!'

Satterlee felt his eyes fly wide. By God! Bannerman was going to do it: draw against a naked, cocked gun!

By God, he was doing it now!

All Satterlee had to do was whip up his Colt and drop the hammer. He did so. The gun blasted but its sound was blanketed by two fast shots from Bannerman's pistol. Satterlee staggered, having instinctively yanked Mariah to one side so he could get a better shot at Bannerman. His big body jerked with the impact of both bullets. He stepped backwards, dragging the girl with him, as his gun fired again by reflex. He went down, Mariah rolling half-across him.

Bannerman stepped around to one side so he could see Satterlee's gun hand.

But he needn't have worried: the gun was on the ground, half-under the girl's sprawled body.

He knelt swiftly when she made no attempt to roll away from Satterlee; then he sat back on his hams, pushing his hat to the back of his head.

'Hell!' he breathed, looking at the spreading blood on Mariah's shirt just above waist level, where Wiley's last bullet had gone in.

★　★　★

Kyle Stanton ran up to the house, calling his sister's name breathlessly.

'Lola! Lola! He's comin'. That gunslinger, Bannister or whatever his name be — an' he's leadin' a hoss with a body draped across it.'

Lola Stanton had been wishing for some kind of interruption, anything to get away from trying to make head or tail of the ranch account books, but she wasn't sure she had meant *this* kind of interruption.

231

But she hurried out to the porch where Kyle was standing, still breathing heavily from his run up from the creek, where he and two ranch hands had been setting up the last of the barbed-wire fencing.

He pointed and she shaded her eyes as Bannerman drifted into the yard, slumped in the saddle, maybe even asleep, as some experienced riders could manage. He was leading a paint with upright black ears and she didn't need to see the clothing to identify Mariah Birdwood, roped across the saddle.

She could also see the blood on Mariah's shirt: a lot of it.

'Kyle, get Ben or Chuck up here to lend a hand. See that Dolores has plenty of hot water. We have some doctoring to do.'

Just then Bannerman lifted his head and they saw the dried blood on one side of his neck and on his shirt.

'Oh, God, sis! I think we better send someone to town for the doctor.'

That was her first thought, too, but something made her hesitate. 'Let's see just how serious everyone is hurt first,' she decided, and Kyle raced away.

★　★　★

Bannerman had been cleaned up. He had looked very bad with all the blood on face and neck, but it had mostly come from his lobeless left ear. It would be sore for a long time but was far from being fatal. Lola had bandaged it well and now he sat beside the bed where a ghastly pale Mariah Birdwood lay. The Stanton girl frowned as she straightened and looked at her brother.

'Kyle, you'd better ride into Laramie and fetch the doctor. I'm afraid Mariah is . . . quite seriously injured.' The boy went out and Lola turned to Bannerman. 'I'm sorry. Mariah needs a doctor. I just hope that afterwards he doesn't spread the word that you were here, but — '

'That's OK,' he cut in. 'I could see

out in the hills that Mariah's pretty bad. Stomach?'

'I — I think so. There's some very serious organ damage anyway. Oh!' She gasped this last as she realized that Mariah had opened her dull eyes and was staring at her. 'Oh, I'm sorry, Mariah! I didn't know you were conscious.'

Mariah nodded slowly, gave a slight twitch of her puffed lips. She shifted her gaze to Bannerman. 'You . . . won.'

He nodded. 'His gun fired as he fell and you rolled across him.'

'It — hurts!' She fought back a sob and two tears rolled down her cheeks. Lola wiped them away swiftly, but gently.

'The doctor will be here soon. Try to stay relaxed. Don't get excited.' She looked at Bannerman. 'Which means no questions, Mr Bannerman.'

He frowned but nodded. Mariah rolled her head on the pillow so she could see him better. 'You . . . want to know what was so . . . valuable to me in that . . . safe?'

'When you feel more like talking, Mariah.'

'I-I may not feel — like it. I — owe it you. I-I made a mistake. If I had been less — arrogant — bossy — I might've had — you for an — ally — a — a protector.'

He said nothing. Lola tried to stop Mariah talking but Mariah was obviously afraid that she was going to die and wanted to say what was on her mind.

'Lola, you have been right — all these years. The dam is mostly on — your land.'

Lola Stanton gasped, her mouth slightly open as she frowned, waiting for this to sink in.

Mariah continued to speak; the survey had been done by the government surveyor, appointed by Washington. His name was Colby, brother-in-law of the wife of Colonel Greer, head of the Territorial Land Agency. Darby Birdwood had seen the possibilities of a large dam that could supply water to the entire basin and the town of Laramie for many years to come. But he wanted control of that water, had sounded out Greer about a deal with Washington: annual payments for 'upkeep' of the dam, renewal of pipelines and so on. These would be grants that required no itemized accounts — when the man in charge, Greer, was a silent partner in the project.

So, survey reports and boundaries were 'adjusted', giving Crown the entire catchment area when actually just under half should have been included on Box S, with more encroaching on the Indian Lands. These 'adjustments' were annually upgraded: 'manipulated' would be a better term, and as the capacity of the dam rose with good years of rainfall, so did the value of the 'grants' made to Crown and its silent partners.

All went well; the Birdwoods were the richest and most powerful ranchers in the County. Colonel Greer saw that all papers were safe from scrutiny by Washington's watchdogs.

Then he was taken suddenly and seriously ill and was forced into early retirement. Heavy rains overfilled the dam and flooded an Indian sacred burial ground. Darby Birdwood was murdered by Indians, from whom he had been stealing for years. Greer had just enough strength to arrange a 'massacre', a total eradication of the tribe in question: men, women, children. There could be no tribe, no land claims. Then he died.

To Mariah's horror, just as she was recovering from her grief over her father's death and things were settling down again, she learned that all Greer's books and ledgers in a certain safe of his office were to be forwarded to the Cheyenne records office; the town had been recently chosen as the county seat and even statehood was hinted at in the near future. So, all records pertaining to Wyoming were to be transferred to Cheyenne, the new county seat.

The security of the army pay-train seemed an ideal time to transport government registers . . .

Once that arrived some bored or nosy clerk was bound to break the seals one day and start reading.

In desperation, Mariah decided that all she could do was set up the robbery of that train. The ledgers might never be missed, would be overshadowed by the theft of the army payroll. Mariah could destroy them at her leisure and Crown would be safe.

Bannerman watched as the doctor worked over her, stood back and shook his head dolefully; there was little hope she would recover.

'She *must* rest now,' the medic said, looking sternly at Bannerman. 'No more questions.'

Bannerman nodded and before the doctor had washed up and packed away his instruments, Mariah opened her eyes, seemed to look briefly up into Bannerman's face, then gasped her last breath.

Lola touched a lace kerchief to both her eyes as the sheet was drawn up over Mariah Birdwood.

* * *

Next morning, drinking after-breakfast coffee on the front porch with Bannerman, Lola said quietly,

'You could stay on if you wanted. We could cover your identity. And there'll be plenty of work.'

Bannerman smiled. 'Thanks, but I'm wanted in a few other places, too. If ever my cover was blown, I'd likely spend the rest of my life on a rockpile.'

She frowned. 'Surely you're not that bad?' He shrugged. 'But — you said you wanted Mariah's money to help a friend, crippled by Wiley Satterlee.'

After a short silence, he said, 'More than a friend. He saved my sister's life and nearly lost his own doing it. I owe him plenty. I have to find her for him, somewhere in New Mexico. She thinks Todd's dead. He let her think that because they were to be married before he was wounded and he didn't want to 'burden' her now he can't walk. But Carmel's stronger than that and I've talked him round. So now I have to find her. The money would've helped but I'll do it anyway — it'll just take a little longer. And there's always work that pays big, if you're not too fussy.'

Her mouth tightened, allowing disapproval to show through as she said, 'I suppose that means more lawlessness?'

'It's . . . a means to an end.'

He could see she was not pleased at this attitude.

'You do something fine and good, then you . . . Well, I suppose you should be moving along, before the army come looking for you.'

When he was ready to go she put out her hand and shook it briefly. 'I won't tell them anything helpful.'

'Don't get yourself in trouble on my account.'

'What will you do? Put your gun up for hire again?'

Her disapproval and disappointment were clear.

He was surprised that it bothered him some, but there was nothing he could do about it. He settled in the saddle and touched a hand to his hatbrim, nodding briefly.

'I'll be ready for whatever comes my way.'

She watched him ride off, lifted a hand as he rode over the ridge without looking back.

'Yes. I guess you're that kind of man, Heath Bannerman. You'll always 'be ready'.'

THE END

We do hope that you have enjoyed reading this large print book.

Did you know that all of our titles are available for purchase?

We publish a wide range of high quality large print books including:
Romances, Mysteries, Classics
General Fiction
Non Fiction and Westerns

Special interest titles available in large print are:
The Little Oxford Dictionary
Music Book, Song Book
Hymn Book, Service Book

Also available from us courtesy of Oxford University Press:
Young Readers' Dictionary
(large print edition)
Young Readers' Thesaurus
(large print edition)

For further information or a free brochure, please contact us at:
Ulverscroft Large Print Books Ltd.,
The Green, Bradgate Road, Anstey,
Leicester, LE7 7FU, England.
Tel: (00 44) 0116 236 4325
Fax: (00 44) 0116 234 0205